A
Candidate
for Murder

A
Candidate
for Murder

JOAN LOWERY NIXON

**Delacorte
Press**

Published by
Delacorte Press
Bantam Doubleday Dell Publishing Group, Inc.
666 Fifth Avenue
New York, New York 10103

Library of Congress Cataloging in Publication Data

Nixon, Joan Lowery.
  A candidate for murder / by Joan Lowery Nixon.
    p. cm.
  Summary: Cary finds her life in danger when she uncovers
a plot to sabotage her father's political campaign for governor
of Texas.
  ISBN 0-385-30257-6
  [1. Politics, Practical—Fiction. 2. Mystery and detective
stories.] I. Title.
PZ7.N65Can 1991
[Fic]—dc20   90-41809 CIP AC

Manufactured in the United States of America

April 1991

10 9 8 7 6 5 4 3 2 1

BVG

For a special friend
NORMA JEAN BACHO

Acknowledgments

With grateful appreciation for their advice and encouragement to political administrative advisers Allie Page Matthews, Deputy Director of Office of Child Support Enforcement, Health and Human Services Department, Washington, D.C.; Donald G. Carlson, Chief of Staff, Office of Congressman Bill Archer, Washington, D.C., and Houston, Texas; and Norma Jean Bacho, Staff Assistant, Office of Congressman Bill Archer, Houston, Texas; to Joe Nolan, Assignments Director, KPRC-TV, Houston; and to Kevin Henry, Director of Security, The Adolphus, Dallas, Texas.

A
Candidate
for Murder

Chapter 1

I stepped out onto the darkened country club terrace and shut the heavy carved door behind me, muting the music and the laughter coming from the ballroom. It was like popping them into a bottle and holding my finger over the top. If I took my finger off—if I opened the door—the noise would blast out like fireworks.

Later, I'd go back, but for a little while I needed to be alone.

I walked over to the railing and leaned on it, taking deep breaths of the warm night air and wishing that Justin were with me. The moon was as slight as a chalk mark, not bright enough to pierce the blackness beyond the terrace; and a pungent bitter-orange fragrance rose from the shrubs below the railing. A setting for romance. But Justin was dancing with Cindy Parker, and I was trying to avoid obnoxious Mark Steadman, who was intent on stalking me with his camera. So what if it *was* Mark's party. He didn't have to be such a dork.

"Hey, Cary! One more!" he'd yelled at me just before I'd ducked into the ladies' lounge to escape. "If your dad gets to be governor of Texas, these candids of you will be valuable."

"Leave me alone!" I snapped, but the flash went off before I could close the door between us.

It was a rotten party, and for at least a few minutes I wanted out, so when I peeked out the door and saw that Mark was busy talking to someone and wouldn't notice me, I slipped out of the rest room, through the hallway, and outside to the terrace.

My thoughts were suddenly interrupted by Mark's booming voice. I turned to see him standing near one of the large ballroom windows, his dark hair in his eyes, his tie crooked. No matter what Mark was wearing, he never seemed put together the right way.

I knew if Mark looked outside he might be able to spot me in the light that spilled through the glass. I slipped out of my shoes and silently ran in my stocking feet across the cool, smooth slate to the place where the terrace makes an abrupt turn as it curves around the dining area. In my shadowed, corner niche I pressed against the wall, trying to become invisible.

A deep voice spoke so close to me that I jumped, ready to run again, but I saw the glowing end of a cigarette arc through the air and fall to the grass, and I realized the man who had spoken was standing just around the curve, his voice carrying in the night's stillness. "There won't be any problem? You're sure of this?"

A second voice answered. It was a strange, scratchy voice that sounded as though each word had been dragged over gravel, then spit out. "Positive. We're back in the ball game—at least as long as the *status quo* doesn't change."

"And it's up to us to see that it doesn't."

There was silence for a moment, and I felt creepy. I didn't like eavesdropping.

The first man said, "I don't mind telling you, I was worried. I never thought Gil would—"

"Well, now he won't. You could say that because of his big mouth, he's up a creek." His chuckle was as rasping as an emery board scraping a broken fingernail.

The door to the terrace was shoved open, and Mark bounced through. "Cary?" he yelled. "I know you're out here. Lee saw you. Where are you?"

Feeling as guilty as though I'd been caught snooping on purpose, I stepped from my dark corner, waving my arms as I tried to signal Mark to be quiet, but it was too dark for him to get my message. He caught only a shadowy movement and galloped toward me.

"There you are!" he shouted.

"Mark!" I warned. "Be quiet!"

I could hear approaching footsteps on the side terrace as Mark aimed his camera and said, "Gotcha!"

The brightness of the flash blinded me. "Mark," I pleaded as I rubbed my eyes and tried to see. "You're not funny."

"I'm not trying to be funny," he said. "If your dad gets to be governor, I'm going to sell these pictures of you. Maybe to *People* magazine."

"Go jump," I muttered. I stumbled into my shoes and stalked toward the door to the ballroom. There was only silence behind me, but I didn't dare look around to see if the two men on the terrace were watching.

Mark trotted after me. "Justin's looking for you," he said. "I'll help you find him."

"I can find him myself!" I threw open the door and plunged into the noise, and the brightness, and Justin's arms.

"Where were you?" he asked.

"Hiding from Mark," I answered.

"How about a picture of the two of you?" Mark asked, and before we could answer, the camera flashed again.

"No more pictures." Justin looked down on Mark. "Unless you want to eat your camera."

"Okay, okay," Mark said and grinned. "That was the last one on this roll anyway." He laid his camera on a small, carved table near the terrace doors, and zeroed in on the buffet table.

Justin smiled at me. "Slow music, Cary," he said. "Come on. Let's dance."

I melted against him, my arms around his neck and my head against his shoulder. I closed my eyes as we swayed back and forth in rhythm with the leisurely beat.

Justin is tall and maybe a little too thin, with red-orange hair and freckles. He might not be the best-looking guy at school, but I don't care. He looks great to me, and he has a super sense of humor. We laugh at the same things and like the same movies—even the same things to eat. I love being with Justin. In fact, I think I love Justin.

When the music stopped I pulled back, smiling, but I

4

could see beyond Justin to the terrace door. It was slightly open, and just outside, barely discernible in the shadows, was a large, stocky man dressed in a dark blue business suit. He squinted as he peered from face to face. It took just an instant before his gaze met mine, and he stopped as though he'd been hunting for me. His look was so intense that his eyebrows drew down into a frown.

I didn't know how to interpret it. Was he angry? Was it my imagination, or did he even look a little scared?

Justin was following my gaze. "Who's that?" he asked.

The man drew back, closing the door behind him.

"I don't know," I said.

"That was some look he gave you. I wonder what's bugging him."

"Maybe he was one of the men on the terrace," I said, and explained, adding, "I didn't mean to listen in, but I couldn't help it."

Justin glanced in Mark's direction and mumbled, "Mark can really be a nerd."

At the moment I wasn't concerned about Mark. I shivered, remembering the strange expression on the man's face. "The way that guy looked at me was scary," I told Justin. "What I did wasn't that bad. I wasn't listening in on purpose."

"Maybe the men were talking about something top secret," Justin suggested.

I made a face. "What have you got in mind? C.I.A. and spies?"

He laughed, then said, "What *were* they talking about?"

"I can't remember much about it," I told him. "Some guy was giving them problems. I don't think what they said was important, and I didn't understand it anyway."

"If that guy at the door was one of them, then he's just an old grouch," Justin said. "Don't worry about him, Cary. You'll never see him again." He looked toward the buffet table and added, "I'm getting hungry. Are you?"

"Yes," I said, and tucked my hand in Justin's as we made our way to the buffet table. Justin was right. The guy was just an old grouch. Forget him!

Later, when I came in, Mom raised her head from the pillow to ask sleepily, "Was it a good party, Cary?"

Justin's good-night kiss was still warm on my lips, and nothing else mattered. "You know it," I said.

I looked toward Dad's side of the bed, but it was empty. "Dad hasn't come to bed yet?" I asked. "It's awfully late."

"I came upstairs about eleven thirty," Mom told me. "Charles was still meeting with his campaign managers."

"There weren't any cars in front of the house," I said. "They must have gone."

Mom sat up and swung her feet to the floor, wiggling her toes into the slippers next to the bed and turning on the lamp on the bedside table. "He's been working too hard on this campaign. I'd better go down and remind him that he needs his sleep."

She pulled on her robe as she walked toward the open door into the hall, and I followed her.

Dad's campaign. I thought of Mark and the way some of the kids were acting. "It's kind of hard to get used to the idea of Dad running for governor," I said. "It makes everything so . . . so different."

Mom put an arm around my shoulders and gave me a quick hug, resting her cheek against mine. "There'll be some changes in our lives," she said, "but most of them will be interesting and exciting."

I smiled and hugged her back without answering. Dad had announced his candidacy three days ago. Since then the phone had hardly stopped ringing, our house was usually filled with people I'd never seen before and whose names I couldn't remember, Dad had been missing sleep, and Mark had been even more of a nerd than usual. Interesting and exciting changes? I had my own opinion about that.

Early Sunday afternoon people began arriving, and I couldn't get out of the house fast enough. I smiled and nodded and shook hands, glad that they all were too busy to want anything more from me. Some of the faces were familiar, but there were new ones, too; and everyone was talking about television slots, telephone appeals, speaking tours, and all the stuff that has to do with a political campaign.

My best friend Allie's house was a safe haven. Allie and I swam in her pool, listened to the music on a couple of new discs, and talked and talked—about the party some, but mostly about guys.

Joan Lowery Nixon

Allie's mouth is a little too big, her nose is a little too long, and she's at least two inches taller than any of the other girls in our class. No matter how many times Allie's mother reminds her, Allie slumps, and if a dish crashes in the school cafeteria we can be pretty sure who dropped it. If we'd been given grades a few years ago when we took the Neiman Marcus class on good manners for preadolescent young ladies, Allie would have flunked, and what's more, she wouldn't have cared. But in spite of being a klutz, Allie's one of the best-liked girls at Gormley Academy—where we go to school—maybe because life almost always looks good to her and she isn't uptight about anything. I always feel good when I'm with Allie.

Allie's mother came out to the patio carrying a phone. "The call's for you, Cary," she said.

I raised my head from the chaise lounge where I'd been tanning. "I wonder what Mom wants."

"It's not your mother," Mrs. Richards said. "It's a boy."

"Justin?" I wondered why he'd call me here.

As her mother walked back into the house, Allie grinned at me and whispered, "Just pretend I'm not listening in."

I took my finger off the mute button. "Hi, Justin," I said.

But it wasn't Justin. "I suppose you think what you did was funny!" someone shouted in my ear.

"Who is this?" I asked.

"It's Mark," he said.

I wondered what was bugging him. "Oh, Mark, your

party last night was great. Allie and I were just talking about how much fun . . ."

He interrupted. "Sure, sure, great party. You showed me how much you liked it."

"What's the matter with you?" I asked.

"You know."

"No, I don't. I really don't."

"I want my film back," he said.

"What are you talking about?"

"You weren't the only one on that roll," he said. "I took a lot of pictures of the party, and I want them back."

I took a deep breath. "Listen to me," I said. "I'm beginning to figure out what you're talking about. Someone took the film out of your camera, and you think I did it."

"I *know* you did it. You or Justin."

Now it was my turn to be angry. "We didn't touch your camera, and we didn't take your film! And I don't like being accused of stealing!"

He began to simmer down. "I—I didn't say *stealing* exactly. I mean, I thought you might think it was funny to take the film, but it isn't."

"We didn't do it."

There was a pause and this time his voice was almost pleading. "You were the only one who got mad about having your picture taken, Cary. Nobody else did. If you didn't take the film, then I don't know who else to ask. I really want my film back. I haven't got any other pictures of my party."

I calmed down, too. "Maybe one of the guys just

wanted to kid you," I told him. "You'll probably find the film in your locker tomorrow."

"You think so?"

"Sure. This all has to be a joke of some kind. Why would anybody want the film for any other reason?"

"I guess so," he mumbled. His voice became more hopeful as he added, "Cary, if you hear anything . . . I mean, if you find out who . . . I want my film back."

"If I find out anything about it, I'll let you know," I said. I hung up the phone, placing it on a nearby table, and said to Allie, "I don't know why anybody would play a joke on Mark. He can't take it."

"He's pretty much of a nerd," Allie agreed.

I felt a little guilty. After all, we had all gone to his party, hadn't we? And a lot of his other parties over the years. "He tries to be nice," I said. "He's really not so bad. He can even be kind of fun sometimes."

"Sometimes," Allie said and raised one eyebrow so high it wiggled.

I couldn't keep from giggling. "Well, anyway," I told her, "I hope whoever took Mark's film gives it back."

"I wonder if he got a picture of Bitsy in that awful thing her mother brought her from Paris," Allie said. "It's a Claude LeBlanc, but it was all wrong for Bitsy. She looked like an African polar bear."

"There aren't any polar bears in Africa," I said, and rolled over on my stomach, laughing.

"Well, a walrus, then," Allie said. She went on with a crazy story about Bitsy's run-in with one of the science teachers at Gormley, and I laughed until there were tears in my eyes. I put Mark and his missing film completely out of my mind.

When the sun began to go down, I knew I had better get home and finish the report that was due in history.

"See you tomorrow," I told Allie, and climbed into Mom's blue Cadillac, which she sometimes lets me use.

I've had a driver's license for months, and I wish I had a car of my own, but Dad said, "Don't even think about it until you're a senior." Dad sometimes says he runs a tight ship, and he's not talking just about his oil company.

As I drove out of the circular drive in front of the Richardses' house, the car's headlights turned on automatically, but it wasn't so dark that I couldn't see the car that pulled from the curb behind me, its lights off.

At first I expected the driver to notice he was driving without lights, but he didn't, so I flicked mine a couple of times as a signal. But his lights stayed off, and his car stayed the same distance behind me. I cut down the nearest side street and picked up speed. When the car without lights did the same, I was positive I was being followed.

This had never happened to me before. I was so terrified that for a moment I grew dizzy, and the shadows and shapes of trees and houses wavered and blurred.

"Hang on," I told myself out loud and took a couple of sharp, deep breaths. "Don't let go. You can handle this."

Okay. Sure. I'd handle it. But how? What was I going to do?

Chapter 2

Was it my imagination, or was the car closing in? I tromped down on the gas pedal, and the Cadillac shot forward as I headed for the traffic on the nearby boulevard. These neighborhood streets were dark and quiet, and I wanted people around for safety.

As I reached the boulevard the traffic light was just changing, but I managed to squeal around the corner before it turned red. From the sound of horns and the screech of brakes behind me I knew that the other car had made it through the light, too.

I had to slow, and I dared a glance in the rearview mirror. The car that tailed me had its brights on now, creating such a glare that I wasn't able to read the license number or see what the driver looked like. All I could make out was a dark, broad silhouette which was definitely that of a male.

I gripped the steering wheel so hard my hands hurt, frantic to have people around me, to have people between me and whoever was in the car behind me. In the next block was a busy shopping center. At the nearest end was a large, well-lit full-service gas station, and that's what I aimed for.

I shot past two cars which were in line for the pumps and brought the car to a halt in front of the office. I didn't stop to look back. I jumped out of the Cadillac and ran inside the station office.

A muscular middle-aged man in grease-stained khakis looked up from the battered desk on which he'd been leaning, studying a map. He marked his place with a dirty finger and tried to hide the irritation that showed on his face as he asked, "What can I do for you, girlie?"

I clung to the frame around the plate-glass window and studied the cars outside. "Someone was following me," I said.

He straightened up and peered through the window. "Is he still out there?"

"I don't know," I said. "I don't know what he looked like."

"What about the car? What make was it? What color?"

"I don't know that either," I told him. "It was dark. Maybe dark gray or dark blue—something like that."

"Did you get a license number?"

"No."

The impatience had returned to his face. "Are you sure somebody was following you? There's a lot of cars out there. You coulda imagined it."

He thought I was an air-head, and I felt myself blushing. *I* knew that someone had been following me, whether this man believed me or not.

14

"Could I use your phone?" I asked.

"Local calls only," he said.

"It's local. I want to call my father."

Grudgingly, the man nodded toward the phone on the desk, and I dialed my home number.

"Don't be busy, don't be busy," I said over and over to myself, and when I heard the phone ring I sagged against the desk with relief.

Dad answered on the second ring.

In a rush of words I told him what had happened, and where I was, and he said that he and Dexter would come immediately to get me.

As I waited for them I stared out the window, eager for Dad and Dexter to drive up. Time stopped moving, and it felt as though they were taking forever.

A month ago Philip, who had worked as our handyman, butler, and sometime chauffeur, left us to move to California. Dad had replaced him by hiring Dexter Kline, who moved into the apartment over the garage. Dexter's pleasant enough, but he has an odd, faded look: pale eyes, pale skin, pale hair; and for a large man he moves very quietly. He isn't awfully good at being a butler, although he's better than when he first arrived and didn't seem to know what he was supposed to do. He's not good at fixing things either. When the pipe broke under one of the bathroom sinks, Dad had to show Dexter what to do with it until the plumber got there. But Dad seems happy with Dexter's work. Maybe he likes Dexter because Dexter's a serious kind of person, and Dad's a serious person, too.

"Oh! There they are!" I burst out as Dad's black Mercedes pulled into the gas station. I flung the door open and raced to meet Dad, who had stepped out of the car even before it had come to a full stop.

I climbed into the Mercedes with Dad, and Dexter followed us in Mom's car. As Dad drove I told him what had happened, and he said, "Are you sure it wasn't a coincidence? The driver could have been taking the same route you did."

"He turned when I did."

"Was the street you took a direct way of getting to the boulevard?"

"Well . . . maybe," I admitted. "I guess it is."

"So anyone else could pick that route, too."

"Yes."

Dad thought a long moment, then said, "This person didn't try to close in or force you off the road, did he?"

"No." I was beginning to feel stupid about the way I'd acted. "Maybe because you're running for office . . ." I couldn't finish the sentence.

Dad gave me a quick glance, which surprised me. He's the kind of person who never takes his eyes off the road. "Honey," he said, "our family has always been in the public eye. We've taught you to take precautions, and we've tried to keep a protective eye on you, but it's been important to your mother and to me that you never live in fear."

"I know," I said.

Dad reached over and took my hand, giving it a comforting squeeze before releasing it. "Cary, I don't want you to start worrying about what might happen. Many people run for office, and their families are perfectly safe."

I forced myself to smile at Dad, even though I wanted to hide against his shoulder and hang onto him tightly, the way I did when I was a little kid and afraid of the dark. Maybe Dad was right that nothing bad would happen, but in my mind I could still see that car following me, and I knew that it wasn't a coincidence. The driver had to have some reason for trying to frighten me.

Mom's questions were almost identical to Dad's, and she finally said she was satisfied that there was nothing to worry about, although every now and then throughout dinner I caught her sneaking looks at me as though she were afraid I might disappear.

I ate fast because I had that history paper to write. I went up to my room, sat in the middle of my bed with my notes spread around me, opened my notebook, and got to work.

I must have been awfully tired, because the sudden, shrill blast of the telephone sliced into my dreams like a scream. I let out a yelp as I scrambled across my bed to snatch up the receiver before it could ring again.

Still half asleep, I mumbled, "Hello?"

A woman answered me. Her voice was low and slurred, and at first I couldn't tell what she was saying. I thought I heard her say my name, but I couldn't be sure.

"I beg your pardon?" I asked.

"You beg my pardon?" she said mockingly, each word

17

slow and careful. She made a snuffling noise that could have been a laugh or a cry, and her voice dropped. "I asked you, what do you know about it? What do you know?"

"I don't understand what you're talking about."

"If they think you don't know nothin' you'll be all right. You don't know, do you?"

It was pretty obvious from the way the woman's conversation rambled that she was drunk. She hadn't called me. She thought she was talking to someone else. "You have the wrong number," I told her.

"You're just a kid," she said, and she started to cry.

"You dialed the wrong number," I said. "Hang up and try again."

I put the receiver back in its cradle and slid off the bed, tugging my rumpled T-shirt and jeans into place. I tried to gather my history papers, which were scattered on the bed and the floor. So much for leaving my report until Sunday night.

I sat on the edge of the bed and stared at the phone. What if the woman did dial again? What if she dialed this number? Her words stayed in my head, and I could still hear what sounded like *Cary Amberson.*

But why would she be calling me? Why would she ask me what I knew? It didn't make sense.

I sat there maybe five minutes before I began to relax. She wasn't going to call, I reassured myself. But I felt uncomfortable, even a little scared. *Had* the woman said my name?

I needed to talk to someone about the call. I needed to talk to Mom or Dad.

The door to my parents' bedroom was closed, which meant that Mom was probably asleep, and the lights were still on downstairs, which told me that Dad hadn't come upstairs yet.

I winced as I stepped on the squeaky board just outside my bedroom door and hurried down the stairs as quietly as I could, thankful that the thick gold-colored carpet absorbed the sound of my footsteps. I raced across the entry hall and down the short hallway leading to the library, where Dad would be working.

He was bent over his desk, writing in the greenish-gold puddle of light from his desk lamp. As he looked up, his eyes widened in surprise. "Cary?" he said. "I thought you were asleep."

"I was," I answered and smiled. "I fell asleep while I was writing my history report, but I got a phone call, and it woke me up."

It was late, and yet my father looked as he always did, tall, good-looking, and dignified, in total command, without a single blond hair out of place. It was a different story with me. As I'd passed the hall mirror I'd caught a glimpse of myself and wasn't happy with what I'd seen. My long light-brown hair looked as though it had lost a battle with my blow dryer, my right cheek was still marked with red lines from sleeping on top of the wrinkled quilt, and my eyes (their bright blue color was the one great thing I'd inherited from my father) were puffy and red-rimmed.

"It's pretty late for your friends to call."

"It wasn't one of my friends," I said. "It was a woman saying some weird things."

Dad slowly laid down his pen and took off his glasses, never taking his eyes from my face. "Here . . ." He pointed to the chair across from his desk. "Sit down. Tell me about it."

I did as he suggested, facing Dad across his wide desk as though I were one of the officers in his oil company there to discuss business. It was a formal setting, but Dad's a formal kind of person. It's hard for some people to understand Dad. He's even been accused of not having a sense of humor, but that's not true. It's just that he doesn't laugh at a lot of silly stuff, and he's never been very good at telling jokes. He wouldn't laugh at a comic who slipped on a banana peel. He'd be more concerned about whether the person was hurt, because Dad is a kind, loving man. And he's smart. He was smart enough to keep his company going during the oil bust back in the eighties, at a time in which a lot of independent companies folded.

When I had told Dad everything I could remember about the conversation, he said, "It's most likely that the woman dialed your number by accident."

"That's what I thought." Dad had said just what I'd hoped he'd say. I felt a thousand times better.

"However," Dad went on, "since you think you heard her call you by name . . ."

"*If*," I said.

"*If* you did, it's possible that somehow she had come into possession of your telephone number."

"But my number's unlisted," I complained. "It's my own private line."

"A person's privacy is never totally protected," he

answered. "Human nature being what it is, there can always be slipups."

I leaned back in my chair and grumbled, "Okay. Supposing the woman really did want to talk to me. Why? What she said didn't make any sense."

Dad leaned back, too, and rubbed his chin. "Cary, honey, I'm sorry, but crank calls like that one seem to be part of the game of politics. At least, that's what I've been told. I'd hoped that our home phones would be protected, and anonymous callers would simply phone the Amberson Company, but apparently that's not the way it's worked out."

"Are you telling me that crank calls have come to your office?"

"I'm afraid so," he said.

The dark shadows that licked the edges of the room shifted and moved closer. I shivered and hugged myself, trying to rub warmth back into my upper arms. "You mean just because you want to be governor, crazy people are going to come after you?" I asked.

Dad explained patiently, "No one's coming after me. There are a certain number of unbalanced people in the world who enjoy making strange telephone calls. A detective with the police force explained that people of this type get their satisfaction out of just making the calls. They usually don't do anything to cause physical harm."

"When did you talk to a detective?"

"Delia took a threatening call. She was frightened and called the police."

I could just picture Delia coming unglued. Delia was Dad's personal secretary at his Amberson Oil Company, and now that his campaign headquarters had been officially opened in a vacant store downtown on Commerce Street, she'd been put in charge of the volunteer staff.

Delia usually fussed over me. She fussed over herself, too, but her strawberry-blond hair color was as fake as the smile she always gave me, and I didn't like her.

I was getting sidetracked. "Dad, if someone threatened you, shouldn't you and the police take the call seriously?"

"There's nothing to worry about," Dad tried to reassure me. "People who make calls like that have so much bottled-up anger it has to spill out somewhere, so it does through anonymous threats and obscenities."

"And you believe the detective? Are you sure that all these crazy callers want to do is talk?"

Dad looked tired, and a frown wrinkle flickered between his eyebrows. "Cary," he said, "all I can do is repeat the detective's assurances that crank callers are usually harmless." He shifted in his chair. "Look, honey, it's late, and I have a great deal of work to finish."

"Okay, Dad," I said. I got up, walked around his desk, and bent to kiss his cheek before I headed back to my bedroom. It really was late—almost midnight—so I quickly washed my face, pulled on the oversized T-shirt I sleep in, and climbed into bed.

My gaze was drawn to the telephone as I turned off my light. *"Don't ring,"* I told it. *"Please don't ring."*

I wouldn't let myself think about the woman who had called. She was drunk. She was a nut. She was history.

But the whisper of her words slipped through my mind. *Cary Amberson.* She had said it. I knew she had called me by name.

Chapter 3

Dad had already eaten breakfast before I came downstairs the next morning. It dawned on me that last night was one of the first times I'd been able to talk to Dad alone since he'd filed for the governor's race.

I helped myself to some of the scrambled eggs and toast that Velma Hansel, our housekeeper, had brought to the table, and sat down opposite Mom.

I know everybody's supposed to think of their mothers as old, but I've never been able to do that with Mom. She always looks terrific, even when her hair is out of place, even when she isn't wearing makeup. Dad says that Mom still looks just like she did when she was in college. Of course, he has to be exaggerating, but Mom likes to hear it. I've never seen her in the courtroom, but if I were on a jury, and Mom were one of the attorneys on a case, I'd give her points just for the sharp, confident way she looks and moves and talks.

Mom wasn't confident this morning. She sat slumped over the open newspaper, just staring, not reading it. She'd mumbled a "good morning" at me when I came in and kissed the top of her head, and I hadn't thought anything of her mumbling, because Mom's always like that when anyone catches her in the middle of reading something important. But this was different. As Mom looked across the table at me, her face was pale, and the skin was tight around her eyes and mouth.

"Mom, what's the matter?" I asked. "Are you sick?"

Mom shook her head. "It's so unfair," she said.

"What's unfair?"

Mom stabbed at an editorial cartoon with one finger, so I got up and hurried around to her side of the table, leaning over her shoulder to see it.

There was a cartoon of Dad. Anyone could tell it was Dad, and yet it didn't look just like him, because the cartoonist had turned down Dad's lips in a sneer. His nose was in the air, his eyes were half-closed, and there was a crown on his head.

"What's he supposed to be sitting on?" I asked, and then I saw it was a throne made out of a tangle of tiny oil derricks and pumpers and tank trucks and dollar signs.

I gripped Mom's hand, and she held mine tightly. "Dad's not like that!" I knew my voice was too loud. "He's running for governor because he wants to do a good, honest job, and that's not what we've been getting. He doesn't want to be a king, and he isn't a snob! That cartoon is a lie!"

There was more I could have said, but Mom folded the newspaper over, got up, and put her arms around me. "There's a lot we'll have to get used to, Cary."

"It hurts, Mom," I said. "It hurt you, too. Your face was so white it scared me."

26

"Well, yours is red," Mom said. "We must make a funny-looking pair."

We both tried to laugh, but it didn't come off. "Sit down and eat your breakfast," Mom told me. "You'll be late for school."

"I don't feel like eating."

"Cary," she said, "going hungry won't solve the problem. There'll be many more attacks like this, and we'll have to get used to them."

"That's not something I want to get used to. I hate reading lies about Dad," I said, but I did pull out my chair and sat down.

"You're going to hear a lot of things that aren't true." Mom leaned over to give me a quick hug. "Don't let it get to you, honey," she said. "We have to keep up a good face. How we react and what we do is going to reflect on Charles."

"Good advice, but that means you, too, Mom." I forced myself to smile, trying to make it easier for both of us.

"You're right," Mom said. "I'll have to practice what I've just been preaching."

Just then Velma opened the door from the kitchen. Her hair was more gray than blond. It was pulled up into a knot on top of her head and anchored with two barrettes which matched her extra-large-size pink blouse and slacks. "Oh, there you are, Cary," she said pleasantly. "You and your mother sound so much alike, now that you're gettin' older, sometimes I can't tell if it's the two of you or if your mother's talkin' to herself again."

Mom looked surprised. "Talking to myself? You make it sound pretty bad, Velma."

"You know what I mean," Velma said. "It's when you sometimes like to read your lawyer stuff aloud." She smiled at me. "Want anything else for breakfast?"

"No, thanks," I answered, but I still had questions for Mom. As Velma shut the kitchen door I asked, "Why is this newspaper attacking Dad?"

"They support the other party. It's a matter of politics," she said.

I shook out my napkin so hard I nearly knocked over my glass of orange juice, but I grabbed the glass in time and managed to get the napkin spread across my lap before I answered. "It should be a matter of truth, not politics. Doesn't anybody care about the truth?"

Mom reached across the table and placed a hand over mine. "Honey, it's not as cut-and-dried as that. To begin with, people have to find out the truth, and that's what a campaign is all about." She smiled and added, "That reminds me—Charles told me you're going to do volunteer work at headquarters."

Mom has always called Dad *Charles,* and he's called her *Laura,* but for the first time it struck me how much this tied into Dad's formal attitude. Didn't they ever call each other nicknames? I tried to think of Dad as a *Charlie* or a *Chuck* or a *Bubba* and almost laughed. Not Dad. He was definitely a *Charles.*

"I want to work in the campaign office every afternoon after school," I said.

"That may be too often," Mom told me. "Your homework comes first."

"But I want to help Dad."

"Eat your eggs," Mom said. "We'll talk about it."

I shoved a forkful into my mouth and chewed automatically. The eggs were cold. I saw Mom give a quick glance at her watch so I said, "Do you want to talk later? Do you have to leave?"

"I have to meet with the people at the center, but I've got a few minutes," she told me. I knew what she meant by "center." Mom gave a lot of volunteer time and free legal work to the rape crisis center. Her work there meant a lot to her. Sometimes she put it ahead of legal work she'd be paid for.

I persisted in my argument, trying to lay it out rationally. I found out a long time ago that being rational got points from a lawyer-mom. "Dad wants me to work at the office, doesn't he?"

"Of course he does," Mom said. "It's just that we're concerned about your being there every day. We're afraid it's going to take up too much of your time."

"I'll get my homework done. I promise."

"The time you'll spend at campaign headquarters has to come from somewhere. What's going to happen to your social life? To your dates with Justin?"

"Mom!" I began before I saw the twinkle in her eyes. "I thought you meant it," I said. "I didn't know you were teasing."

She laughed. "I wasn't teasing about the homework, Cary. You understand that it has to come first?"

"I promised it would."

The teasing look in her eyes returned. "Maybe Justin will come in and work with you," she said. "What a romantic setting . . . counting bumper stickers, making countless telephone calls."

I polished off the last drop of orange juice and said, "No kidding, Mom. I really am going to ask Justin if he'll come in and work after school with me, at least a couple of days a week. Allie told me she might be able to."

Mom looked at her watch again, stood, and pulled a suit coat over her light blue silk blouse. "Your father is going to take you to school this morning," she said as Dad came into the room.

"I've got an appointment, Cary, so we'll have to leave early," he told me. "Five minutes?"

"I can make it," I said and raced upstairs to collect my books. I'd be glad when no one had to drive me back and forth to school.

Dad was sitting patiently in the car when I dove into the front seat beside him. "Okay," I said. "So it was *six* minutes."

"Six-and-a-half," he said, and we both laughed. Dad *did* have a sense of humor. It was just a lot more quiet than everyone else's.

We'd had an early fall cold snap, a blue norther that had swept down in time to color the leaves of the Chinese Tallow trees, which now dusted the landscape with faint shadings of gold and red. But the temperature had climbed back into the eighties, so I adjusted the nearest air-conditioner outlet, enjoying the chill as the cold air blew directly on me. Dad had the radio turned to a station I liked, but as the music ended the disc jockey said, "I've got a couple of good ones for you

. . . Did you hear that Charles Amberson is so rich that the last time he cashed a check the bank bounced?

"And when Amberson was asked what he planned to do for homeless people if he became governor, he said, 'Homeless? Then obviously, they need to be put in touch with the right real estate agents.' "

I felt the blood rush to my face, and I clenched my fists. "You didn't say that! The whole thing is a lie!"

Dad reached out and snapped off the radio. "Everyone knows that. Those were supposed to be jokes."

"They weren't funny!"

"I agree." Dad paused a moment, then said, "This isn't going to be easy for any of us."

I slumped back against the seat. "Why do you want to go through all this? Grandpa left you his oil company, and managing it is a big job, so why run for governor?"

"I've talked about my reasons with you, Cary," Dad said. "I feel strongly that the people of Texas shouldn't be shortchanged by a governor whose bank accounts are growing at their expense."

"Then why don't you just try to have Governor Milco arrested or impeached, or whatever it is you do with crooked politicians?"

"It isn't that simple. The investigation would have to go through channels, and criminal intent would have to be proved. There'd be other people involved who'd do everything in their power to cover up any evidence which might hurt them, too."

"You make them sound dangerous."

Dad shook his head. "Don't borrow trouble. Governor Milco will play by the rules."

What kind of rules did a crooked politician play by? I searched Dad's face, but his expression didn't tell me anything. All I knew was that I didn't feel as confident as Dad seemed to be.

We were halfway to Gormley Academy when the car phone rang, and Dad answered it.

The conversation was brief. Dad suddenly slammed down the receiver and picked up speed. "What's the matter?" I asked. "Where are you going?"

"To the scene of an accident." Dad's voice was tight and raspy as he answered, "A part of the new state highway collapsed. Two workmen were trapped and probably killed."

Neither of us spoke as we drove to the scene. Dad had to park his car a short distance away—the other side of a deep and narrow creek, its banks overgrown with shrubbery, that ran under the new highway. He strode toward the accident scene, and I trotted along after him, trying to keep up. We could see a couple of collapsed concrete and steel piers lying under a large, broken, concrete slab. A body, covered with a sheet, lay near the paramedics' ambulance, and workmen were digging frantically, shouting instructions to each other. Two television crews were already on hand, both of them broadcasting.

As Dad and I arrived at the cordoned-off area, one of the workmen stood and wiped sweat and tears from his eyes. His voice was flat as he said, "No use. Ortiz is dead."

He stumbled to a place on the grass near us, where he

dropped to his haunches, pulled a rag from his pocket, and mopped again at his face.

Dad tried to duck under the yellow police tape, but a uniformed policeman quickly warned us away. Dad told him who he was and showed some identification, but that didn't help. "Stay behind the lines," the policeman ordered.

The workman heard Dad give his name and looked up at us. "You the Amberson who's runnin' for governor?" he asked.

"Yes," Dad said.

"You said you was lookin' into some of the construction contracts. That right?"

"That's right."

"Okay," he said. "I hope this one's on your list. These people in charge—I suspect they're cuttin' down. Not enough steel, maybe too much sand. I hope you find out what's goin' on and tell it like it is."

"Can you give me proof?" Dad asked.

The man shook his head. "I'm nobody important. You get yourself an engineer. Take samples." He lowered his voice. "There was a supervisor here, name of Herb Gillian. He didn't like the way things were going, and Cragmore fired him. I don't know where he moved off to, but see if you can find him. He'll tell you what you need to know."

A young man wearing a business suit and hard hat strode over, his lips pressed into a thin angry line. He immediately snapped an order to the worker. As the worker slowly dragged to his feet he turned to Dad. "Find him," he said.

With a screech of tires a third television truck rolled up. A reporter hopped out—a youngish woman I'd often seen on TV. She gave a quick glance around, saw my father, gestured to a cameraman, and the two of them rushed to join us. I heard the reporter give a few opening statements, and as Dad began to speak, a microphone was quickly thrust in his direction.

"What is your name and your position here?" Dad asked the man in the hard hat.

There was so much authority in his voice that even though the man blustered and sputtered indignantly, he stammered, "I-I'm G-Gerald Lockman. I'm with the Cragmore Construction Corporation." His glance flicked back and forth between the reporter, the cameraman, and Dad. He managed to straighten his shoulders, glared defensively at Dad, and said, "I see no reason why you should be here, and I have no intention of answering your questions."

Dad ignored Mr. Lockman's rudeness. "I'd like your permission to enter the area," he said. "I'd like to talk to some of the workmen."

"No!" Mr. Lockman spit out the word, then—with one eye on the camera—struggled to get himself under control. "As you can see, we've had a serious accident. Unauthorized persons on the scene will only add to the problem."

The reporter squeezed closer, stepping in front of me, and asked Gerald Lockman, "Can you tell us how this accident happened? Was the Cragmore Corporation to blame?"

Mr. Lockman took a step back, tripped, and nearly

fell. "I'm not authorized to make a statement," he said. He turned his back on Dad and the reporter and hurried away.

The reporter, seemingly afraid Dad would also leave, shoved the microphone into his face. "Mr. Charles Amberson," she said. "You've made statements about alleged problems in the construction industry. Is that why you're here? Does this accident somehow tie into the construction problems?"

Dad said, "As I said in my speech when I announced that I was a candidate for governor, my staff and I are compiling records that will show that during the past three years many low bids on construction projects have been ignored, with contracts awarded to the same small group of contractors at a much higher cost to taxpayers."

I'd heard Dad mention at home that these contractors had been heavy contributors to Jimmy Milco's initial campaign for governor. I wondered why he wasn't telling the reporter that now. Maybe he was saving it for the big speech he'd talked about—the one he'd give at the fund-raiser banquet in November.

"Are you saying that Cragmore Construction got this job through political favoritism?" the reporter asked.

"There were two companies with lower bids. I have copies of those bids, although the records Governor Milco made public did not include those two companies."

The other two TV reporters had arrived with their cameramen, and one of them shouted out, "What has this accident got to do with your allegations about the bids?"

As they held out their microphones I stepped back, out of the way.

"First," Dad said, so unruffled I wondered how he could manage it, "I'm requesting that samples from this scene be tested, that impartial engineers be sent here to examine the site."

The original reporter asked, "Are you implying that this was *not* an accident?"

"Of course it was an accident," Dad told her. "I'm simply requesting that authorities determine the reason why this accident happened."

I heard the screech of brakes and turned to see a large, stocky man jump out of a white Jaguar. His shirt sleeves were rolled up, and his tie was loosened at his neck so that it sailed over one shoulder as he ran toward us. I recognized him immediately. It was the man I'd seen glaring at me through the outside door of the country club ballroom, the man I'd guessed must have been one of the two I'd overheard on the terrace.

He elbowed his way through the group until he was face-to-face with Dad. His voice was hard as he declared, "This isn't your territory or your concern, Amberson."

Microphones were thrust forward, the reporters listening intently as Dad said, "It's the concern of the people of Texas, Cragmore."

So that's who the man was—the owner of this construction company.

A thin, balding man in a brown suit opened the door

in a mobile office that was parked nearby, and stood just inside, listening and picking at a dark spot on one side of his chin.

I heard Dad say, "For the record, I'm going to request an official investigation into the quality of materials being used in the construction of this overpass."

Mr. Cragmore's face flushed red, but he was very much aware of the cameras and reporters. He took a deep breath and said, "You're fishing, Amberson. Your only reason for being here at the scene is to get a little glory for yourself."

I was furious! "That's not true!" I yelled.

Mr. Cragmore wasn't sure who had spoken up. He stared with surprise at the reporters, as though one of them had said it.

"Cary!" Dad said, looking as though he'd temporarily forgotten I was with him. "I'd better get you to school. You're going to be late."

Mr. Cragmore didn't answer me, but I knew he remembered who I was, and I hoped he could tell that I recognized him, too. Jerk! To talk like that to my dad!

Dad nodded toward the reporters. "Thank you," he said. "I'll prepare a statement, and my campaign manager will see that you get it as quickly as possible." Clasping my hand, he strode toward his car.

I ran to keep up with him, taking two steps to his one.

As we passed the mobile office, the man at the door turned and said to someone I couldn't see, "I don't care what you do. Get those reporters out of here."

It was the same strange, rough voice I'd heard on the country club terrace.

I froze, tugging my hand from Dad's, and stared at the man in the brown suit.

His eyes met mine, and the wary expression on his face told me he was aware that I had recognized him.

The door closed with a bang as Dad asked, "Cary? What's the matter?"

I just wanted out of there—as fast as possible. "Come on, Dad," I said, running ahead. "Let's get in the car."

Once we were inside I asked him, "Did you see the man who was standing inside the door of that trailer?"

"No," Dad said. "What about him?"

"He was at the country club with Mr. Cragmore. I overheard them talking about business and about staying in the ball game. I don't remember most of it because I didn't understand it."

Dad shot me a quick look. "Then what are you getting at?"

"Well, if they're in business together, why did the man in the trailer act like he didn't want to be seen?"

"I have no idea," Dad said, and I knew his mind was on the accident and on what the worker had told him, so I was quiet and let him think.

I had things to think about, too. Those men—Ben Cragmore and the other one. There was something about them that scared me.

Chapter 4

Dad was somewhere in his own thoughts as we drove to school, so we didn't talk, but as we pulled up in front of Gormley Academy and I opened the door on the passenger side, Dad reached over and rested his hand on my arm. "I hope I can make things clear to you, Cary," he said. "As you know, Governor Jimmy Milco is one of 'The Good Old Boys.' He's firmly entrenched with long-time supporters. The best way—probably the only way—to stop Milco from what he's doing is to put him out of office. That's what I'm trying to do. You understand that, don't you?"

"I understand," I said.

I hopped out of the car and walked briskly across the grass. The first bell would ring at any moment.

The campus was crowded—a sea of blue slacks and skirts and white shirts and blouses, the school uniform —but I had no trouble finding Justin. Tall people stand out, especially tall people with red hair. Justin was say-ing something, and at least half a dozen kids were crowded around him, leaning in to hear him with grins on their faces. Justin has a great sense of humor and was probably entertaining them with another new joke. I ran up behind Justin, but the group was so intent on what he was saying, no one noticed me.

"So he says, 'Homeless? Then obviously, they need to be put in touch with the right real estate agents.' " As Justin delivered the punch line, everyone laughed.

I tried to take a deep breath, and my heart began to pound. Justin was my friend—more than a friend. How could he do this to me?

One of the guys in the group spotted me. He stopped laughing and nudged Justin, who whirled to face me, guilt creeping over his face.

I hate you! I thought, so suddenly and furiously angry that I wanted to stomp on his feet and kick his shins and beat him over the head with my history book!

"Oh, Cary," Justin said. His smile was shaky with embarrassment as he stammered, "Hi. I didn't know you were here."

The hurt made my throat and chest ache, but I remembered Mom's warning. The way we react will reflect on Dad.

"Hi," I forced myself to say and smiled as though I hadn't overheard a word. "I just got here. Everybody was laughing. Something funny?"

"Uh—just a joke," Justin said. The bell rang, and he let out such a huge sigh of relief it would have been laughable if I hadn't known the reason behind it.

The group broke up as everyone left for class. Justin put an arm around my shoulders as we walked, bending his head in order to speak just to me. "Can I come by again after school?" he asked, his voice so low and soft that my anger began to melt.

I'd always been honest with Justin, but I'd pretended I hadn't heard the joke, so now I was stuck with my deceit. There was nothing else to do but go on as though nothing had happened.

He nuzzled the top of my head with a kiss, and that settled the matter. I smiled up at him. "You can give me a ride after school, if you want to."

He squeezed my shoulders. "You know I want to."

"But not home," I added as we stopped outside my geometry classroom. "I'm going to work at Dad's campaign headquarters."

"Oh," he said, and his glance slid away.

I took one of his hands in mine and said, "Come work with me. It'll be fun."

Justin didn't answer.

"Well?" I asked. I guess I was slow to figure things out, but I'd been so sure he'd want to.

He looked back at me, and his skin behind the freckles was flushed. "Your father's a real nice guy and all that, but if I—uh—worked for his campaign, well that would be—uh—committing myself, wouldn't it?"

Now it was my turn to be embarrassed. "I-I guess so," I stammered. "I hadn't thought about that part."

Justin took a moment to get things under control and said, "Cary, let me think about it. Okay?"

"Sure," I said, but I was disappointed and more than a little hurt. Why'd he have to make such a big deal about it? Couldn't he do it because of me?

The hallway was almost empty. "You'd better go," I

said, "the bell's going to ring any second." Before Justin could answer, I turned away and hurried into the classroom.

The bell clanged just as I slid into my seat. Mrs. Trimble raised an eyebrow and gave me one of those *you lucked out* looks, but Allie, who sat across the aisle from me, sent me a grin and a wink.

I wanted to tell Allie what Justin had said. I needed to talk to someone who'd care. But Mrs. Trimble isn't the kind to waste a minute, so we were immediately plunged into proving theorems, and I forgot all about Dad's campaign.

However, after class Allie brought it all back to me.

"My Dad said he'd kill me if I worked on your father's campaign," Allie told me as we walked together to history class, "and I believe him. He takes his politics seriously."

I stopped and stared at her. "You mean he won't let you make up your own mind?"

Allie wasn't the least bit flustered. "Cary," she said, "my mind will belong to me when I'm twenty-one, of legal age, and all that. Right now it belongs to my father's bank."

"Bank?" I didn't understand.

"Bank, as in two board members being on the opposite political side from your father."

"Oh," I said, feeling stupid. "I was just thinking about you and me, not anyone else."

Allie just smiled. "You wouldn't really want me to help at the campaign office," she said. "I'd do all right with the phone calls, but I'd probably get all the bumper stickers stuck to each other and mess up something important."

"Yes. I guess you would."

We laughed, and Allie rattled on. "Say, that's what I should do. I'll volunteer to work for one of your dad's opponents. That would be the best help I could give you. Which one will it be? So far, I think there are three in your dad's party, counting your dad, who've filed for the primaries, although according to Daddy—and don't quote me!—your father's by far the best qualified." She lowered her voice, stuck out her chin, and frowned as she imitated her father. "My guess is that Amberson's going to take the damned primaries."

"Which candidate are the bank directors for?"

"Oh, glory, none of the above! The directors are Good Old Boys. They'd never vote any way but their straight party ticket because their daddies did, and their granddaddies did, and if they didn't too, there'd be such a rollin' over in the graveyards that people hereabouts would think Texas was having an earthquake."

I giggled. When I was down, Allie could always make me feel better. I told her about asking Justin to work at headquarters with me and how he'd reacted. "I guess he may be getting some family pressure too. I understand."

"Sure. That's it," Allie said, her voice hearty.

But it wasn't.

During lunch period Justin avoided me, so after school I was all set to call home and ask Dexter if I could take the car or—if he needed it—ask if he'd drive me to

Dad's campaign office. I was on my way to the telephone in the attendance office when I heard Justin call me.

I turned and waited until he caught up. He was going to come with me. Good.

But Justin took my arm and pulled me aside, out of the path of the kids who were heading toward the lot where their cars were parked. His eyes were dark with concern as he said, "Come on. I have to take you home."

I tried to tug away from his grip. "No!" I insisted. "I told you. I'm going to Dad's campaign office."

"Cary, please," Justin said. "Listen to me. You can't go there now. Not after what's happened. I have to take you home."

Chapter 5

I was so scared that my legs wobbled and I gulped air as I tried to talk. "What's the matter, Justin? Tell me!"

"Wait till we're in the car," he said and half-guided, half-dragged me out of the building and across the lot to his white BMW. Inside, he twisted to face me and said, "I called home to tell Mom I was going to be late because, well, I was going to work at your dad's office with you."

He paused and gazed down at his hands, rubbing at an imaginary spot on the steering wheel. "Look, Cary, you've got to understand. I mean there are a lot of jokes about Charles Amberson, and who he thinks he is, and all that, and I know I should have told you right away that I'd help on the campaign, but I didn't want the guys to make fun . . . ."

His voice broke into a mumble, and I reached out and grabbed his shoulders, shaking him as I turned him toward me again. "That doesn't matter! I want to know what you were talking about. Why can't I go to Dad's office? You said, 'after what happened.' Tell me *now*. Did anything happen to Dad?"

Justin looked surprised. "No one's hurt, if that's what you were thinking."

"Then what is it?"

"Well, reporters might still be there, and I'd just as soon keep you out of it."

"Out of what?" I was shouting, but I couldn't help it.

"Okay, okay," he said. "Calm down. I'm trying to tell you. My mom was listening to the news at noon, and she heard that this morning somebody broke into your dad's campaign office over on Commerce Street and sprayed paint around and ruined a lot of stuff."

I groaned and asked, "Who did it?"

He shrugged. "Mom said no one knows."

"Justin, please take me to the office," I said. "They'll need my help more than ever."

"They'll just tell you to go home."

"Either take me to Dad's office, or I'll go back to the school and call Dexter," I said.

"Okay. If that's what you want," Justin answered. He turned the key in the ignition, drove out of the parking lot with a bump and a screech of tires and headed toward the expressway.

We got a good look at the damage in the large front room of headquarters through the wide plate-glass windows that used to be a storefront. Bright banners and posters still hung over the top of the windows and door, but they seemed incongruous now and out of place. No one from the news media was at the office when Justin and I arrived. The big story was over, and this was only the aftermath. The office was like a hollow shell without the crowds of people who'd been in it since the first day it was open. Dad was there. Mom, too, along with Delia, and a man who was a stranger to me. The four of them stared helplessly at the blue splotches on the desks and chairs, the phones, the computer, and the stacks and stacks of papers. Behind them, thin blue lines dribbled down the far wall.

Delia was the first to notice Justin and me, and as she raised a hand in greeting the others turned and looked at us. Delia was standing next to an old, bald, stocky man who, even in this warm weather, wore a buttoned-up vest that stretched and gaped between each tattered buttonhole. He blinked at me, and his eyes shimmered behind thick glasses.

Always proper, always correct, Dad shook hands with Justin, introduced him to Delia, and took my arm. "Cary, you haven't met Mr. Sibley," Dad said. "Edwin, may I present my daughter, Caroline, and her friend, Justin Willis." To me he added, "This is Mr. Sibley's first day as one of our volunteers."

We shook hands and greeted Mom and Delia, and it struck me as odd, with this frightening mess around us, that we should behave as properly as though we were at a dinner party.

"Where is everybody?" I asked.

"We sent them home," Dad said.

"I'll go home, too, and change," I said, "and come back and help clean up."

Dad shook his head. "Thank you for offering, Cary,

but we've hired a professional cleaner to take on this job. It's going to be even more difficult than it looks."

I surveyed the room again and shuddered. "Do the police have any idea who might have done this?"

"It was my fault." For the first time Edwin Sibley spoke up without mumbling, and I saw that the reason his eyes seemed to shimmer was that there were tears in them.

"Nonsense," Dad said.

But Mr. Sibley persisted. "When I signed up yesterday, they told me they'd need more banners, so I volunteered to get here early and paint some, but I stopped so I could run down to the little snack bar near the corner and buy a Coke. I should have put the paint away, but I left the can on the desk and the door unlocked."

"No one else was here?" I looked toward Delia.

"Well, I was, of course," she said. "I had the responsibility of unlocking the office for Edwin, but at the time he left for the store I was in the restroom." Her nose and cheeks grew red and she clipped each word, not wanting to have to answer to me. "And I didn't hear a thing."

"None of us needs to take the blame," Dad said.

"The police think some kids may have done it," Mom added. "They could be right. Some kids hanging around downtown could have seen Edwin leave the office, tried the door, then spotted the paint can." She held out her hands to the room. "You can see the result."

I was disgusted with the creeps who had made this mess. "It's so frustrating!" I said.

For the first time since the introductions, Justin spoke up. "If we can't help around here," he said, "I'll drive Cary home."

"Thank you, Justin," Mom said. "That's a good idea." She gave me a kiss on the cheek and said, "We'll see you at dinner, honey."

I followed Justin to his car, climbed in, and leaned back against the seat with a sigh.

He gave a comforting pat to my knee and said, "I'm sorry all that happened, Cary, but don't get discouraged. They'll get everything fixed up soon and be back in business."

I didn't answer. I was wondering if I should tell Justin about my weird phone call. Dad had said that people who made those calls didn't do anything, but with this paint-spray thing happening the day after the call I wasn't so sure Dad and the detective were right. What had the woman said? Something about "if they think you don't know" . . . Know what? Who were the "they" she was talking about? What would they do?

I'd just about decided to confide in Justin when he suddenly said, "Why don't we talk about something else —something important? We're running out of time. The Halloween dance is less than a week away."

I stiffened. "That's what you think is important? A Halloween dance?"

The car made a little wobble. "I mean it's important because we've got to decide what kind of costumes we're going to wear."

"I can't believe you think that's more important than what happened at Dad's campaign office!"

"Cary," Justin said, his voice rising too, "I was just trying to change the subject. What's done is done. It's over. Okay?"

"Okay," I snapped.

For a few minutes he was quiet. Then he said, "What's wrong with you, Cary? One of the things I like the most about you is the way you laugh at things instead of letting them get to you."

"This is different."

"No, it's not. You're different."

"That's dumb. What am I supposed to do—laugh because Dad's office was trashed?"

"You don't understand what I mean."

"No! You're the one who doesn't understand!"

Justin drove his BMW into our residential area and automatically dropped his speed as he passed the rows of huge old mansions, which seemed to stare down at us demanding proper behavior. Neither of us spoke until the car swung into the long curving drive that leads to my house.

He brought his car to a stop so suddenly I was bounced forward. "When you're in a better mood we'll talk," he said.

I climbed out and slammed the door, knowing he hates it when anyone does that, and ran into the house, tears beginning to blind me. I wanted everything to be just as fine as always between us. Why did he have to ruin everything?

Velma came into the entry hall, peered out the window as Justin drove away, and gave me a careful look. "Oh-oh," she said. "Looks like somebody had a fight with her boyfriend."

I wiped away my tears with the back of one hand. "It doesn't matter."

"That's the way to look at it," she told me and smiled. "There'll be lots of boyfriends in your future."

But I didn't want lots of boyfriends. I wanted Justin.

The kitchen smelled wonderful, with browned beef juices and herbs and seasonings. We were going to have another of Velma's marvelous stews.

Forget Justin. I wasn't going to let what he said get to me. "Yum! That smells great," I told Velma, and she gave me a big smile.

"I've got some apples and those red grapes you like all washed and ready to eat," Velma told me. "They're in a bowl on the bottom shelf of the refrigerator."

"Thanks," I said, but I helped myself instead to a couple of fat chocolate marshmallow cookies from a package I'd put in the freezer to get hard. When I'm unhappy I don't feel like being healthy.

The phone rang, and Velma sighed. "That phone's been ringin' itself off the hook all afternoon," she told me. "I wonder where Dexter is. He's helped me answer when he's had a chance. We got a long list of messages for your father."

As she answered the call I went upstairs to change into shorts and a T-shirt.

I had no sooner pulled the shirt over my head and stuffed my mouth with tough, chewy marshmallow than my own telephone rang.

By the third ring I had managed to gulp down the mouthful of cookie and said, "Hello."

There was a pause. "Hello," I repeated, but no one answered.

I was about to hang up when I heard a familiar voice ask, "Is this Cary Amberson?" It was the woman who had called me last night.

"Yes. I'm Cary," I answered.

The woman cleared her throat, and I could hear her breathing, but she didn't speak, and after a while I couldn't stand it.

"Do you want to talk to me?" I asked her.

"I've been thinking," she said. "There's just some things I can't take. I don't want you to get hurt."

I shivered with the cold that crawled up my backbone. "What are you talking about?"

"Maybe you don't know, but if you figured it out . . . You see? They can't be sure. They don't know if they can take the chance."

In the background I heard a man call out, "Nora?" The woman gave a little squeak, and the line went dead.

I sat on the bed, trying to calm down by thinking it out. Who was Nora? What was she trying to tell me, and why had she been in such a hurry to hang up? She acted like someone who was afraid, but what did that have to do with me?

Was Nora just one of the crazy, crank callers Dad had talked about? She had to be. We didn't know any Noras. Drunk or sober—and this time I guessed she was sober —what she had told me didn't make any sense. She was some strange weirdo who had managed to get hold of my unlisted telephone number, and I told myself I'd be as goofy as she was if I let myself get frightened by her calls. I'd tell Mom or Dad about Nora, and then I'd forget about her.

I polished off what was left of my cookies and went back to the kitchen to get a soft drink.

Velma had been listening to the Channel 13 newscast, but as I pulled a cola from the refrigerator and popped the can, she turned down the volume and said, "They said your father's office got trashed."

"That's right. The police think it was just some kids with a spray paint can."

Velma shook her head slowly. "I sometimes wonder what this world is comin' to," she said. "Bad kids causin' so much damage. It's sad. It's truly sad. When I was growin' up in Beaumont, we'd never have got away with anythin' like that. Why, my cousin Billy Joe . . ." She went on talking for another ten minutes about her cousin's comeuppance when he got in trouble dropping water balloons on people passing under the church steeple.

I was finally able to end the conversation by mumbling "homework." I gathered my books from the hall table and walked toward the stairs. In spite of my decision to put Nora out of my mind, I found myself trying to figure out who Nora was and what she wanted.

From behind the staircase in the entry hall someone suddenly stepped forward, and I gave a yelp before I saw that it was Dexter Kline.

Dexter moved so silently he could come into a room

and I wouldn't know he was there, and when he spoke I'd jump, just as I had now.

"I didn't mean to startle you," he said in his soft, low-pitched voice.

"It's okay," I reassured him. "I didn't hear you come in." How many times had we said these same words to each other?

"Your mother called," Dexter said. "She's with a client and asked if dinner could be a half hour later than usual. She asked me to inform you that if you'd prefer, you could be served dinner alone."

I began to wonder, was Dexter really this formal all the time, or did he act like this because he was trying to be a good butler? What was Dexter really like?

It dawned on me that Dexter was waiting patiently for my answer. "Oh . . . I-I'll wait and eat with Mom and Dad," I said.

Dexter gave a little nod. He went toward the kitchen, and I trotted up the stairs, my thoughts turning back to Nora. *I don't want you to get hurt,* she had told me, but she hadn't said enough.

Who was it who wanted to hurt me? And why?

Chapter 6

Dad and Mom were quieter than usual when they arrived home for dinner, about five minutes apart. Dad's shoulders drooped, and there were dark gray shadows under Mom's eyes.

Mom looked around the dining room as she entered and her eyebrows lifted in surprise. "Don? Ralph? Nobody's with you?" she asked Dad.

"I insisted that I needed some time alone with my family," he said and held out Mom's chair for her.

"I'm surprised they agreed."

"I didn't give them a choice."

Dexter, dressed now in a white coat, entered the dining room, carrying our salad plates. Mom thanked him, and Dexter glided silently out of the room.

"Did the cleaning company work out?" Mom asked Dad. "Poor Edwin Sibley took it awfully hard." She shook out her napkin and laid it across her lap.

"The office is fine now," Dad answered, "and the last time I saw Sibley he was hard at work." He smiled. "I've got some good news. It looks as though we'll get some campaign support from Senator Bowins."

"Wonderful!" Mom said.

"By the way," I asked, "who's Edwin Sibley?"

Mom looked surprised. "You met him."

"I think Cary means, what is his relationship to the campaign," Dad said. "Mr. Sibley is a volunteer."

"What I really mean is, what does he do? What is he like? What kind of a job does he have? All that stuff. Do you know him? Have you worked with him before?"

"No," Dad said. "You'll have to ask Delia about him."

"Shouldn't you know all the people who work in your office?" I asked.

Dad shook his head. "That would be ideal, but impossible." He studied me. "Why all the questions about Mr. Sibley?"

"I was thinking about the blue paint," I said.

"You don't suspect Mr. Sibley, do you?"

"I don't know. Oh, I suppose not. He's a little strange, but I guess he's all right," I said, "but what if you get somebody really weird who comes in and wants to work for your campaign? Do you just tell them *no thanks*?"

"You can't do that," Dad said.

Mom stepped into the conversation. "I can answer that one," she said. "A few years ago I worked for Betty Aldrich when she ran for the United States Congress. We took all the helpers we could get and were glad they were there, but once a woman came to the office whose behavior was somewhat strange, and we were all a little afraid of her. Connie, who was managing the campaign office, gave her such boring work to do that the woman finally gave up and didn't come back."

"The office manager couldn't just tell the woman not to come?"

"You have to be subtle," Mom said. "Candidates for all offices badly need their volunteers, so volunteers are treated royally. You can't afford to offend anyone."

I wondered, what if a volunteer weren't just strange? What if the person might be dangerous? How polite do you have to be to someone who's a threat?

There was silence for a few moments while we ate, but Dad suddenly started and said to Mom, "I'm sorry. I should have asked. How did the depositions go?"

She sighed. "It was a difficult afternoon. The defendant's attorney has an attitude problem."

Thank goodness neither of them remembered to ask me about school. Ten points off on my history paper because it hadn't been finished on time. I'd have to do makeup work to keep my semester grade high. At least the paper was written now, and I had it ready to hand in tomorrow.

Dexter came in again, took the salad plates out, and brought the entree. After a few more unsuccessful attempts to start a conversation and keep it going, Mom and Dad both ate slowly, lost in thought.

I studied Dad, and I tried to put myself in his place. Running for governor was not something he'd thought up overnight. He'd talked a lot about it to Mom and sometimes to me, stressing the extra work, the heavy job of campaigning for the primaries and—if he won in his party—the even more demanding campaigning that would have to be done in order to win the job of Governor of the State of Texas. Knowing how thorough Dad always is, I was sure that he'd tried to think of all the pluses and minuses. But I wondered if he'd even imagined the hatred and ridicule and insults that would be flung at him.

They hurt Mom and me. They must hurt Dad too. I chomped down on part of a broccoli spear. Dad was a nice guy. What good did it do the D.J. to make up a joke about Dad saying or doing something he didn't say or do—all of it a lie? Was bashing Charles Amberson worth it just to get a laugh? Did the cartoonist feel extra clever because he'd made fun of Dad? I knew that their careers depended on how funny they were, but I've never thought that being mean was funny.

I couldn't tell Dad about the second phone call from Nora. He had enough to worry about. However, as soon as I got the chance, I was going to tell Mom.

That chance came soon after dinner. Dad went into his library to meet with Don Franklin and Ralph Dolan, who were managing his campaign, and I followed Mom upstairs and into the master bedroom.

The room didn't match either Mom or Dad. Both of them were businesslike, and the suits Mom wore each day were simple and tailored. But their king-sized bed was covered with the softest of comforters, and the gleaming ivory sheets were made of satin. The pair of armchairs next to the bookcases at the far end of the room were upholstered in rose velvet, and there were lace and velvet pillows everywhere. The bedroom looked as though it had been designed for some glamorous blond movie star. Was this Mom's fantasy world?

Mom tossed her blouse and skirt on the bed, stepped into her robe, and zipped it up. "What are you smiling at?" she asked.

"I was thinking that your bedroom belongs on a movie set."

"And that it's a little out of place for a career woman and an oil company president?"

"Well . . ."

She laughed. "When I was young, there was very little money to spare. My aunt made our sheets herself out of heavy muslin, so they'd wear longer. I'd roll over, my elbows sore from that rough, scratchy fabric, and I'd dream of the kind of bedroom I'd have when I grew up. I read in a magazine about a movie star who had satin sheets and little decorative pillows covered with real lace, and I decided that was what I wanted."

"So this is your childhood dream come true?"

"Exactly, and I love this room, because it's proof that you can work to make dreams come true." She yawned. "I'm going to take a long, soaking, hot bath," she said, "and try to forget what happened to Charles's campaign office."

She waited politely for me to leave the room, but I perched on the edge of one of the velvet chairs and said, "Mom, could I talk to you first?"

"Of course," she answered and sat in the chair opposite mine.

It had always been like that. No matter what kind of a day Mom had been through, all I'd had to do was say, "I need to talk," and she was ready to listen. I knew how tired she must be and how much she really wanted to be left alone, but this had to be said.

"I had a couple of strange telephone calls," I said. "They were from the same person."

"I don't like that," she said. "Maybe we should ask the phone company to put a tracer on your phone."

"I don't think the caller is just some weirdo," I told her. "The first time I thought she said my name, but I wasn't sure, because she sounded drunk. This time she asked if I was Cary Amberson."

I could see Mom tense. "What did she say?"

"Not much. It seemed hard for her to talk to me. For a long time she didn't say anything. Then she told me there were just some things she couldn't take and she said, 'I don't want you to get hurt.'"

"What did she mean by that?"

"I don't know. She rambled around. She said something about how I might figure it out. Nothing she said made any sense to me."

"Did you ask her what she meant?"

"Yes, and I think she was going to tell me more, but I could hear a man call her. She made a funny little noise and hung up."

Mom leaned forward. "Did the man call her by name?"

"Yes. Nora."

"I don't know anyone named Nora. Do you?"

"No," I said.

"We'll talk to the police about the calls, of course," Mom told me.

I felt kind of sick. "Mom, do you think this woman is real? That someone's really planning to hurt me?"

"Nobody's going to hurt you, Cary," Mom said, her voice firm. "You said the woman was drunk."

"Only the first time."

"What she told you didn't make sense in either call, did it?"

"No."

Mom took my hands and held them tightly. "We'll keep her from bothering you again, honey."

"How?"

"We'll have the telephone company change your phone number."

"I never thought of that!" I was so relieved I laughed. "Oh-oh! That means I'll have to give the new number to Allie and Justin and . . ."

Mom stood and reached out a hand, pulling me to my feet. She wrapped me in a quick hug before she teased, "Cary, my love, will you please, *please* let me take my bath now?"

"Sure," I said. We smiled at each other, and I left the room, but as soon as the door closed my smile vanished. I'd thought of a lot of friends I should give my new private number to—friends who knew the number I had now. Was this how Nora got my phone number? Through someone I thought would keep it private?

I started down the stairs, and as I reached the landing I saw Velma standing at the foot of the stairs. "There you are, Cary," she said. "Thank goodness I don't have to climb those stairs to tell you someone's here to see you."

Joan Lowery Nixon

"Who?" I asked, immediately hopeful.

"The boyfriend," Velma said in a loud stage whisper, and my heart gave a jump. "Come to make up, I imagine, 'cause he brought you somethin'."

Now the smile on my face was for real. I galloped down the stairs and into the living room where Justin was waiting for me.

He held out his arms. One hand dangled a small grocery sack. "Peace offering," he said. "Ice cream. Your favorite. Double chocolate chunk."

I laughed and wanted to run right into his arms, but Velma had followed me into the room.

"You want me to dish that up?" she asked.

"No, thanks," I said. "We just need two spoons. We'll eat the ice cream out on the patio." It was the perfect place to be on a warm night with the spicy fragrance from the nearby banks of gold and red chrysanthemums, the hum of a few late cicadas in the elm trees, and only a soft blue glow from the underwater lights in the pool to break the darkness.

Velma brought us two long-handled spoons and turned on the outside lights that spotlighted the patio. As soon as she'd gone inside Justin turned them off. We nestled into one of the porch swings and shared the ice cream and a few chocolate-flavored kisses.

"I'm sorry about the way I put things," Justin murmured against my ear. "I didn't mean them that way. I know how important your father's campaign is to you. If they want us to work in the campaign office tomorrow, I'm ready."

"Thanks, Justin," I said and added a kiss. A little later

62

I told him, "I shouldn't have got so angry. I'm sorry about the things I said. You're right. We have to start thinking about what kind of costumes we're going to wear to the party."

The patio lights flashed on, so brightly that we squinted.

This time it was Dexter, who announced, "It's time to lock up now. Besides, it's late and Cary has school tomorrow."

Justin smiled as he got up and pulled me to my feet. "How many parents have you got?" he asked.

Too many, I thought. I didn't mind when Velma got a little bossy, but I didn't like it when Dexter took it upon himself to tell me what to do.

As I walked with Justin to the front door he said, "See you at school tomorrow."

"Thanks for the ice cream," I said and reached up for one more quick kiss before we had to say good night.

As soon as I'd climbed into bed, I snuggled between the sheets, pulled the blanket to my chin, and immediately drifted into sleep.

It must have been very late when, mingled with my dreams, I heard the rumble of men's voices at the foot of the stairs as Dad said good night to his visitors. And it was even later when I became aware of the slow, exhausted thump of his footsteps as he climbed the stairs to bed.

Chapter 7

Dad's charges did get covered in the newspapers and on television, along with Ben Cragmore's denial, but a political columnist, who'd been taking potshots at Dad, wrote a sarcastic story about Dad visiting the scene of the accident only because his advisers sent him and described Dad as being very careful not to get too close so that he wouldn't get his thousand-dollar suit and handmade Italian shoes dusty.

I looked at the picture of the writer next to his column. "This guy wasn't even there," I said. "How can he get away with a lie like that?"

Before either of my parents could answer I said, "I know what you're going to say—it's politics. But please, *please* don't say it!"

"Don't pay attention to that column," Dad said. "The collapse of the freeway is being investigated, so the truth will come out."

"If someone's actually going to print the truth, how will anyone recognize it with all this other stuff being written?" I asked.

"Cary," Mom said, "don't sound so cynical. Your father's right. The truth *will* come out."

I doubted it.

Before I had to leave for school a detective, who introduced himself as Sgt. Jim Slater, came to the house, and I told him what I had told Mom. He asked questions and made notes and said practically the same thing that the other detective had said to Dad about strange people who get their kicks out of making threatening calls but never follow through.

"But the woman didn't threaten me," I said. "It was more like she was trying to warn me about something."

"Just another form of intimidation," he said.

Mom told me that my phone number would be changed during the day, and I went off to school feeling a lot better about the whole thing and looking forward to my first day as a volunteer in Dad's campaign office.

By the time I arrived at the office everything had been put back in order. Every trace of the blue paint was gone, and the room was crowded with all sorts of people. With the exception of Edwin Sibley—who nodded to me from across the room—and two men with good haircuts and well-tailored business suits, all the people in the room were women, from a good-looking girl with long, perfectly straight black hair, who was dressed in shorts and a sleeveless T-shirt, to a small-boned elflike woman with thin blue-white curls who was wearing an expensive black St. John knit with ropes of gold chains.

Each desk was staffed, and people were sorting mail, using telephones, and carrying large cardboard boxes of who-knows-what back and forth from the front room to the offices at the back. I would have liked to get a look at what was in all those boxes. Campaign literature? Posters? Yard signs? Or did things like yard signs come *after* the primaries? There was a lot to learn.

I suppose I'd had a romantic notion about Justin working side by side with me, but Delia had something different in mind. She raised her voice over the murmur of conversation, interrupting it in order to introduce us to the group, and people beamed and giggled and applauded when Delia called me "the daughter of Texas' future governor."

I spoiled it all by blushing. Dad could stay calm and cool with all this attention, but I wasn't used to it. I was trying to think of something nice to say in return when, all of a sudden, everyone went back to work, leaving me standing there with my mouth open. I closed it, feeling even sillier than I'd felt before.

Justin was immediately assigned to move some of the heaviest of those mysterious boxes, and I was led to what must have been the only empty chair in the room, behind a table near the front door, and given a pile of letters and envelopes.

"You'll be working next to Marjorie Lane," Delia said. "If you run into any problems you can ask her for help."

I turned toward the heavyset woman in an expensive dress and loads of jewelry who was seated next to me, but Delia didn't give me a chance to speak.

"Fold each letter in thirds, place it in an envelope, seal it with that sponge thingie, and toss it in the box on the floor," Delia explained.

"What about stamps?"

"We're using a postage meter," Delia said. She didn't have time to answer questions. She went over to talk to the two guys in business suits, and the three of them disappeared in the direction of the back offices.

Once again I tried to say hello to Mrs. Lane, but after the curious appraisal and quick nod of recognition she gave me when I first sat down, she never took the telephone receiver away from her ear. Rapidly, she was checking the names on a long list as she made call after call.

"We're reminding you about the reception tonight at seven P.M. at the Hotel Adolphus. While all three of our party's candidates will be honored, we hope you'll give your support to Charles Amberson . . ." Her voice went on and on with the same message. It was being drilled into my brain, and I'd probably recite it in my sleep.

I knew about the other two candidates for the party's nomination: Edna Poole, who was a judge in El Paso, and Stanley Barker, who was a state legislator from Houston. I'd heard Delia say, satisfaction in her voice, that neither of them had the name recognition Dad had.

Before I started my assignment I did a quick read-through of Dad's letter. It sounded like Dad. It was straightforward and right to the point as he listed his major goals: eliminate graft in the state offices, develop a tough antidrug action, and consolidate some school districts in order to save money and stretch the equality funds even further. Unfortunately, I had to admit to myself that the letter was kind of dry and boring, but I guessed most campaign literature was like that. I wondered how many voters would actually read it.

Boring. It made me remember what Mom had said about the way unwanted volunteers were sometimes gotten rid of, and I wondered if that was why I had been given this job. Fold letters and stuff envelopes, fold and stuff, fold and stuff.

The girl in shorts came over. "Hi," she said. "My name's Francine."

"Hi," I said, grateful for someone close to my age to talk to. "I'm Cary."

"So we've heard." She smiled and added, "This is just like in the movies. The boss's kid starts at the bottom and works up."

"Up to what?" I asked.

She raised one eyebrow and said, "Up to the inside, secret stuff."

"I don't know what kind of secret stuff you're talking about."

"Private investigator stuff. You know, like what one candidate finds out about another one, such as Jimmy Milco."

"Why Governor Milco, in particular?" And why my sudden suspicion over a simple question? Was I beginning to mistrust everybody?

Francine smiled. "It's just the first name that came to mind."

"Well, to answer your question, if my dad finds out anything about Jimmy Milco he won't keep it secret."

"Come on," she said. "You've got your Dad's best interests at heart. Right?"

"Yes, but . . ."

"So there are probably things you know, maybe things you've overheard, that you'd use to help your father, if you could."

She was studying me so intently that I looked away, embarrassed. What was she getting at?

"Nobody gives me any inside information," I told her. "I'm just one of the volunteers."

"Me too," she answered and smiled, but I could tell from her eyes that wheels were still going around and around in her mind.

"Are you in high school?" I asked, trying to change the subject.

"Nope," she said. "College. Political science major, as a matter of fact."

I gestured toward all the volunteer workers in the room. "Then all this should be really interesting to you."

"It is," she answered. As Delia walked through the room, Francine caught her eye and quickly said, "Well, I'd better get back to work." She hurried to one of the desks near the far end of the room.

I looked around for Justin, but he was nowhere in sight, so I went back to my job. Fold the paper, stuff in an envelope, and seal. Fold, stuff, and seal. Fold and . . .

Through the plate-glass windows I saw a young woman in jeans jaywalk across the street and approach the office. She was wearing a light denim jacket and her blond hair was pulled to the back of her neck. She had a shoulder bag and camera case slung over one shoulder, and she carried a notebook. She caught my glance and smiled before she opened the door. "Hi," she said. "It looks a lot different around here than it did yesterday morning."

I smiled back. "Want a job? Try stuffing envelopes. One exciting fun-filled minute after another."

She chuckled, shifted her notebook to her left hand, and held out her right. "I'm Sally Jo Wilson, with *The Dallas Gazette.*"

I shook her hand and said, "I'm Cary Amberson."

One eyebrow rose, and her lips pursed as she took another look at me. "Ah-ha. The candidate's daughter."

"The future governor's daughter," I answered.

"Fair enough."

I liked Sally Jo's smile. It flickered back and forth on her face like a lightbulb that wasn't screwed in properly, and it was so contagious that I couldn't help smiling in return.

"How about an interview?" she asked. She placed her bag and her camera on the floor, pulled a pen from her shirt pocket, opened her notebook, and sat on the edge of the desk.

I hesitated, and she said, "Let's see . . . Caroline Jane Amberson . . . sixteen years old, only child, born in Dallas, as was her father; mother born in Chamberlin, North Dakota; parents met at Southern Methodist University; married in 1972; Caroline Jane attends Gormley Academy, good grades, member of the Booster Squad, played the oldest Trapp daughter last

71

spring when the school put on their yearly musical, has a trust fund in her name—established by her grandfather—and has no police record."

Shocked, I asked, "Where'd you get all that information about me?"

"Easy," she said. "Reporters know how to find out almost anything about anyone. Most of your life is in the public record."

"I don't like that," I said. "How are you going to use that information?"

"It's hardly the kind of exposé stuff that sells the newspapers on the grocery checkout counters, is it?" She laughed, and I couldn't help laughing, too. "Now . . . how about that interview?"

"I haven't got anything to talk about," I told her.

"Talk about your father. What kind of a dad is he? A little stuffy maybe? Does he hate your boyfriends?"

"Come on," I said. "He's not like that at all. He's a great father." I leaned my elbows on the table and looked up at her. "I'm awfully proud of him."

"Describe your father in one word. Or is that too hard?"

I shook my head. "It's easy. The word is *honest.*"

The eyebrow went up and down again, setting off the smile. I was so fascinated with her face I found myself staring.

"Isn't that a descriptive label all the candidates use?" she asked.

"I don't know," I said. "I don't know that much about politics. You asked me about my father, and I told you. He's a totally honest person."

"How about you?" she asked. "Are you following in his footsteps?"

"Of course," I began indignantly, but I started to giggle. "If you don't count a few little white lies."

The smile flashed over her face again. "Everybody tells white lies," she said and made another notation in her notebook before she asked, "How do you feel about the changes it will make in your life if your father wins the gubernatorial election?"

"Changes?" I went blank.

"You know—moving to Austin to the governor's mansion, changing schools, your mother having to give up her law practice—things like that."

Changing schools? Going to a new school in my senior year? Going to school without Justin and Allie? And what about Mom? It hadn't occurred to me that she'd have to give up the job she loved so much. I know I should have thought about all this, but I hadn't, and here was a reporter wanting to hear my answer. I wasn't ready for this. Remembering the phrase I'd heard countless times in television dramas, I took a deep breath, stared Sally Jo straight in the eye, and said, "No comment."

"I thought you were a political innocent," she said, "but that remark's right out of a politician's handbook."

"I didn't know how else to answer. You asked me a terrible question."

"I suppose so," she said. "No one really wants to leave their friends. You've got a boyfriend, too, I suppose."

"No comment," I said again, comfortable with the phrase now. "Some things are private."

We both broke into laughter.

We chatted a few minutes. Her questions were good, and I answered them. Then Sally Jo surprised me with the question, "What do you think of the Milco commercial about your father?"

"I don't know. I haven't seen it."

"It ran on TV for the first time last night. You'll be seeing it sooner or later."

"Is it mean?"

She nodded. "It's hardball."

"Why would Governor Milco run an ad against my father now?" I asked her. "This is just the race for the primaries. They won't be held until March, and there are two other candidates in Dad's party."

"Your father's the front runner. Milco's camp must see him as a threat, or they wouldn't go after him so early. I suppose Amberson could take that as a compliment." She tapped with her pen on the notebook. "Okay, you haven't seen the commercial, but what's your opinion of some of the other media comments about your father?"

"You mean like that ugly cartoon in yesterday morning's newspaper?"

"Yes."

"It wasn't true. It wasn't anything like Dad, and it hurts."

"But editorial cartoons are a part of politics."

"Making fun of people shouldn't be—especially when it's nothing but lies."

"Your father doesn't seem to have any skeletons in the closet, so his opponents will concentrate on any issues which might make him lose points with the voters."

"But that cartoon made Dad out to be a rich snob who doesn't care about anyone else."

"*Rich* is the key word," Sally Jo said. "You'd be surprised how some people can react to that word."

She stooped to pick up her camera, and I asked, "Is the interview over?"

"Not yet," she said, as she stood and focused on me. "Just keep talking. I'm listening."

Sally Jo had taken two quick shots when Mrs. Lane detached the phone from her ear and glanced up, slightly glassy-eyed. She stiffened when she focused in on Sally Jo. "You're from the *Gazette,* aren't you?" she asked. "I saw you here yesterday morning."

"That's right," Sally Jo said. She held out her right hand and began to introduce herself, but Mrs. Lane looked at Sally Jo's camera and at me and began to flutter and stammer and finally said, "You'll have to talk to Delia Stewart. You shouldn't be talking to . . ."

"The unpaid help," I said with a grin, finishing her sentence for her.

No sense of humor. She didn't smile. She rose to her feet, her strands of pearls clattering against each other as they bounced off her chest, and said to Sally Jo, "Will you come with me, please?"

"I'll see you later," I said to Sally Jo.

"Right," she answered. She picked up her things and followed Mrs. Lane to the back offices.

I liked Sally Jo, but I didn't have a chance to talk to her later, because in about fifteen minutes Delia escorted her to the front door and stood like a guard until she saw Sally Jo cross the street and climb into her car.

Then Delia turned to me. "Thank goodness that was the *Gazette,* so we won't have to worry about a partisan slant, but from now on, Cary, I want you to remember that talking to reporters is a no-no," she said sternly, as though I were three years old. "Requests for interviews should come to me, and if I think they're suitable I'll set them up and be right there with you during each interview . . ."

I finished her sentence. "To tell me what to say."

She wasn't sure how to take that remark, but she decided on a patient response. "Not exactly. It's so I can interrupt if you're asked the wrong questions."

"What are the wrong questions?" I was deliberately giving Delia a hard time, and pretty soon steam would probably come out of her ears.

"We'll discuss this later," she said. "I've got more important things to do—like find the postage meter. How could a postage meter just disappear into thin air?"

As she trotted off I reached for another letter to fold and turned toward my tablemate, who had politely stayed out of range while I was being scolded and was now squirming into her chair like a hen settling into a nest. "How did you happen to volunteer to work for my father's campaign?" I chatted, hoping for some conversation to break the monotony.

She raised one eyebrow and looked indignant. "I've always worked hard for the party. Delia can attest to that."

"I didn't mean—" I began, but the phone was already up to her face, and she began reciting, "We're reminding you about the reception tonight at seven P.M. at the Hotel Adolphus . . ."

Edwin Sibley walked past. He was dressed in the same pants, shirt, and buttoned vest he was wearing when I'd met him. I leaned forward, eager to have somebody—anybody—to talk to. "Hi!" I said.

"Hello," he answered, but he ducked his head, avoiding eye contact, and kept going. Was he still blaming himself about that mess with the blue paint?

At five o'clock, right on the minute, Delia rapped for attention, gushed her thanks for everyone's hard work, and begged all volunteers to come to the reception. "Charles and Laura Amberson will make their appearance after everything is well under way, at eight o'clock," she said. "We're getting good television coverage, and we want as many bodies crowded into the ballroom as possible—*all* of them giving loud support to Mr. Amberson."

I winced at that remark. Dad was going to be giving a speech, and I knew he'd been working hard on it. He wanted people to listen and pay attention. He didn't want just a room filled with noisy bodies.

Delia's voice rose a notch higher, and I could hear the excitement in it. "I've got some good news you'll all be interested in. The banquet in November—the big fundraiser . . ." She chuckled as she slowly emphasized each word. ". . . at one thousand, five hundred dollars a ticket—sold out this afternoon!"

People laughed and clapped. I did, too. That wasn't

just good news, it was great news! It scared me to think how much it cost just to run for governor—millions of dollars! Even Dad wouldn't have enough money to handle the expenses alone.

Delia managed to herd us out of the office while she turned off the lights and locked the door. She was working hard for Dad's campaign and seemed to be doing a good job of running the campaign office, but I couldn't help it. I didn't like her.

I flopped against the padded seats in Justin's car, so tired that I ached. "Thanks for coming," I told him. "I didn't know I'd be asking so much of you."

"You should be a guy," he said. "Women take one look at you and expect you to carry all the heavy stuff. Edwin Sibley was the only other male who hung around, and he wasn't much help." Justin rotated his shoulders and rubbed his arms.

I reached over and massaged the back of his neck. He relaxed, closed his eyes, and said, "Mmmmmm, yeah, that feels good."

In a few moments he opened his eyes and looked at me warily. "Are we supposed to go to that reception tonight?"

"No," I said. "Mom thought I'd better skip it. I've got too much homework."

Justin sat upright and looked hopeful. "Homework. That's right. I've got a big paper coming up. How about if we only work at the office every other day?"

"If you don't want to work there at all, it's fine with me," I said. "I thought they'd need a lot of help, but they had a ton of people already helping, and frankly, when I asked you to go with me I could picture us side by side, working together. It was sort of romantic."

Justin laughed and turned the key in the ignition. "I can think of better ways of being romantic."

So could I.

It wasn't until after Justin had dropped me off at home and I had dumped my books on the entry-hall table, as usual, that I realized my shoulder bag was missing. "Oh, no!"

"What's the matter?" Mom asked as she came down the stairs.

"My shoulder bag," I said. "I left it on the floor next to my chair at Dad's office."

"Do you need it before tomorrow morning?"

"Yes, I do. My wallet's in it and my list of homework assignments and all the rest of my stuff. I have to go back and get it."

Mom looked at her watch. "Velma has your dinner almost ready."

"It won't matter if I'm late for dinner. I'll feel better about it if I go for the bag now. People who might look through those big windows into the office could probably see it, and I don't want someone breaking in to get it."

"Do you want me to drive you?" Mom asked.

"No," I said. "You and Dad have that reception to get ready for. If you lend me your car I can take care of this myself. I won't be long."

Mom gave me the car keys and an extra key to Dad's office. It didn't take long to drive downtown, since I was traveling against the rush-hour traffic, but I was halfway there when it dawned on me that I was driving without my license. I drove very cautiously, scared to death I'd make some mistake and get picked up. The last thing I wanted to get was a traffic ticket.

I gave a huge sigh of relief as I parked in the lot next to the office. I'd made it! My mind was on my driver's license, which was in my shoulder bag, as I ran to the front door of the office and opened the door. It wasn't until I was inside, with the door shut behind me, that I stopped hurrying long enough to notice that in one of the back rooms a light was on. I heard a sliding sound, like a desk drawer shutting, and the light was snapped off.

"Delia?" I asked.

I waited for someone to appear in the open doorway, but there was only silence.

Chapter 8

A figure slid from the door into the short hallway as I snapped on the light switch.

"For goodness' sakes!" Francine cried. She leaned against the wall and put a hand over her heart, loudly gasping for breath. "You scared me to death!" she complained.

My first reaction was to apologize, but those gasps were too fake to be believed, and I realized that Francine was trying to put me on the defensive. "What were you doing back there in the offices?" I demanded.

"For that matter, what are *you* doing here?" She walked toward me as she spoke and stopped about ten feet away.

"It's not the same thing," I said and dangled the key to the front door over my head. "I left my shoulder bag here and came back to get it. I wouldn't have gone into the private offices, but that's where you were."

"Big deal," she said.

"How did you get in here?" I asked her.

Her eyes crinkled, and the corners of her mouth

turned up, but there was no humor in her smile. "It doesn't matter, does it?" She picked up a small clutch bag from the chair on which she'd left it and started toward me.

"Don't leave," I warned her. "I think I'd better call Dad."

She surprised me by pulling out a chair and sitting on it. "Go ahead," she said.

I turned to the phone, but as I dialed our number a hand pressed hard against my back, sending me sprawling across the table. The door opened and slammed, and I straightened in time to see Francine running down the street.

Dexter answered and called Dad to the phone. I told Dad what had happened, and he said, "I don't think we need to call the police. Make sure both the front and back doors are locked. Keep the lights on and wait right there. Your mother and I will be with you as soon as possible."

I did as he suggested and dropped the key in my shoulder bag, which was on the floor where I'd left it. The back door was not only locked but bolted. Had Francine been able to get hold of a key?

I tried to remember what the room was like when Delia had announced it was time to lock up. I closed my eyes, and I could picture some of the people and where they were standing, and I could see them pick up their things and cluster at the front door, moving through, then stopping to chat in small groups out on the sidewalk. Many of them walked toward the parking lot, as I did.

But I couldn't put Francine into this picture.

Of course, I had been more concerned with Justin, and I was awfully tired from folding letters for a couple of hours. Had I seen Francine leave and just not noted it? Or was it possible that Francine had hidden in the rest room and didn't leave at all?

I walked past a couple of small offices to the one in which I'd found her and turned on the light. It was Delia's office—a small room with a desk, three chairs, and two file cabinets on the far wall. One of the drawers in the nearest file cabinet was open.

There were two posters on the wall, one with a campaign slogan and the other with an enlarged photograph of my father, just the barest of smiles on his lips. He looked earnest and sincere.

I was beginning to hate the words. They sounded like campaign promises, like something waved around only until after elections, but in Dad's case they weren't. They were the way he really was. I studied his photograph and tried to disassociate myself from it. Suppose I were a voter, a person who didn't know Charles Amberson at all. Would I believe the expression on his face?

A sound at the front door made me jump, and I ran to the hallway. I could see my mother, dressed in a smooth black sheath and pearls for the reception, peering through the window as my father unlocked the door. Mom looked relieved when she spotted me. The door swung open, and I hurried toward my parents.

"I didn't touch anything," I said, "but Francine did.

Joan Lowery Nixon

One of the file drawers is open, and I'm pretty sure she was going through the desk."

"Who is Francine?" Mom asked as she and I followed Dad back to Delia's office.

"All I know is that she's majoring in political science," I said.

"Where?" Mom asked.

I shrugged. "She didn't say."

Dad stopped in the doorway, surveying the room before we entered. "What's her last name?"

"I don't know that either."

We silently and cautiously walked into the room as though someone were going to jump out at us. Mom asked Dad, "She must have been searching for something. What do you think it was?"

"I have no idea," he said.

"Francine said something that now seems a little strange," I told them. "She said I was the boss's kid, starting at the bottom. Then she asked if I'd move up to working on the inside, secret stuff. I didn't know what she was talking about. What's the secret stuff?"

Dad shrugged. "Some of our operational methods, I suppose. Results of our investigations of the governor's questionable tactics. Mailing lists of those who support our campaign. Nothing confidential is kept here. The young woman who was going through the files couldn't have found what she was looking for."

"I wish I knew why she did it," I said. "It couldn't have been for herself. She must have been working for someone."

"Jimmy Milco?" Mom said. "That information you're

84

collecting on the construction—" She stopped abruptly, as though she were afraid to put the rest of her thought into words.

Dad calmly answered, "The girl was probably just a student, as she told Cary, and she may have had some romantic, grandiose ideas about uncovering what she hoped was secret material."

Mom didn't answer, and I didn't think Dad had reassured her any more than he had me. "Aren't you going to see if she stole something from the files?" I asked him.

"Not now." Dad looked at his watch and moved toward the light switch, shepherding Mom and me out of the office. "Delia's the one who'd know if something were missing. She'd also have the list of volunteers and their addresses and phone numbers. We'll put her to work on it tomorrow morning."

"And bring someone in to check for wiretaps," Mom said.

"Yes," Dad agreed. "There's always that possibility."

So . . . he *did* think it could be something more than he was letting on. "Francine was going through your papers," I insisted. "She might even have stolen something. Don't you want to call the police?"

"No," Dad said. "The publicity could create even more of a problem."

By this time I'd scooped up my shoulder bag and we'd reached the front door.

"We'll walk you to the car," Dad said. He locked the door behind us.

I looked back at the well-lit office. "You forgot to turn off the light," I said.

Dad shook his head. "Your mother and I might as well wait there until it's time to appear at the reception. The Adolphus is just up the street, and there's no point in driving all the way home."

I looked at my watch. It was close to seven. "Do you have to wait until eight to show up? Can't you just get to the reception early?"

Mom laughed and gave Dad a wink. "No," she said. "The crowd should be on hand, as well as the television cameras. Grand entrances for candidates are an important part of the political structure."

As we reached Mom's car I turned to give both Mom and Dad hugs. "I hate politics," I said. "It should be simple. People who want to run for office should give their reasons why, and voters should decide which reasons are the best. But there's so much mean, sneaky, lying stuff involved."

Mom still had one arm around my shoulders, and she gave me a comforting squeeze. "Life isn't simple, Cary," she said. "Unfortunately, the way things should be and the way they actually are can be very different. When—*if*—you study the law someday . . ."

I interrupted. I wished I hadn't asked the question. I really didn't want to talk about or think about the governor's race. It was frustrating. Infuriating. "Don't think of me as a future lawyer," I said with a laugh. "Right now I'm trying to decide whether to be a ballerina or a brain surgeon." Grinning at that old joke, I climbed into Mom's car and drove off, leaving them standing together, holding hands.

When I got home Dexter wasn't in sight, but Velma winked at me and said, "That boyfriend of yours called. I told him you'd call him back *after* you ate dinner. I've got it ready for Dexter to serve right now, soon as I can find that man."

Her eyebrows dipped in the barest of frowns as she spoke. I looked from one side to the other, stepped close to Velma, and lowered my voice. "What do you think of Dexter?" I asked.

Her glance shifted to cover every corner of the room, just as mine had done. "He gets his work done," she said. "That's all that counts." She paused just an instant and leaned toward me. "There is one thing. I never can tell when he's nearby. He don't make much noise when he walks."

I nodded. "It's kind of creepy."

She straightened and said matter-of-factly, "I wouldn't say that. It's just that I'm still used to Philip bein' around. Dexter's a lot different."

As soon as I finished dinner I called Justin to give him my new telephone number.

"I've been waiting for you to call," he said. "I was talking to Greg. He and Allie think that the four of us should go to the Halloween party dressed like heavy-metal roadies. What do you think? We could get some of that colored hair spray that washes out and spray a streak in your hair and you could comb it up or something so it would look real weird."

I giggled. "How about you?" I asked. "And Allie and Greg? There are going to be *four* of us looking weird, I hope."

"Yeah," he said. "I've been hunting around, and I've come up with some good stuff. My aunt's got this scraggly, blond, long-haired wig she wore once at a costume party. I can wear it and a ripped black T-shirt with a skull on it and some jeans that are full of holes. What do you think?"

"Sure," I said, caught up in the idea. "I know where I can get a knit miniskirt, and I'll wear black tights with a lot of holes in them and a torn T-shirt. Oh . . . and real heavy makeup. Won't I look great?"

We both laughed, and Justin said, "We're all going to look so tough the chaperons will want to throw us off the dance floor."

We talked for a while, until Justin's mom told him she had to use the phone. Right after I hung up I called Allie, who broke up.

"It kills me," she said. "We'll look so wild it'll drive the chaperons crazy."

I gave her my new number, and we started talking about the party and Justin and Greg—our favorite subjects. But suddenly another voice interrupted. It took Allie and me a couple of seconds to figure out that someone else had cut into our conversation. "What?" I asked. "Who are you?" I'd heard the words the woman was saying, but they hadn't sunk in.

"This is the operator," she patiently repeated. "I have an emergency call for this number. Will you please end your conversation?"

"Right now," Allie said. She hung up, and I stammered, "Y-yes?"

"Hold on, please," the operator said to me, and the next voice I heard was Mom's.

"Everything's all right, Cary," she said over the noisy voices in the background, so I immediately knew everything *wasn't.*

Chapter 9

"Mom!" I begged, scared to death. "Is Dad all right? What's the matter?"

"Cary, please. Just listen," Mom said. "Your father's fine, and I'm fine. I'm calling you only so that you'll be prepared for the ten o'clock news."

"What . . . ?"

"Listen!" she ordered, so I did.

"A man at the reception created a disturbance," Mom explained, "and—of course—the television cameras caught it."

"What did he do?"

"He tried to make his way through the crowd and reach Charles."

"Why? Was he trying to hurt Dad?"

"I have no idea," Mom answered.

"Who was he?"

"I don't know," Mom said, and her voice sounded tired and strained. "It was all a nightmare. People were shouting and pushing, and I didn't hear much of what the man was yelling. It was something about oil companies ruining the ecology."

I realized that I was clutching the telephone receiver so tightly that my fingers hurt. I tried to relax, but I shivered again. "Did he have a gun?"

"No. Fortunately, he didn't."

"Did they catch him?"

"Yes. The hotel security officers were very efficient. It was over in just a few minutes."

"Oh, Mom," I said. "What if the man had been able to reach Dad!"

Her voice was strong enough to keep me from giving in to tears. "I wanted to reassure you before you caught the story on TV."

"Thanks, Mom," I mumbled. Why didn't Dad give this up? Why did he want to do this to himself?

"We'll be home in a couple of hours, honey," she said.

"You mean the party's going on anyway?"

"Of course," she said. "In fact, in just a few minutes your father will be giving his speech." She paused, then said, "Oh-oh! They're starting now. I've got to run."

"Good-bye, Mom," I said, but she had hung up so fast I wasn't sure she'd heard me.

I filled Allie in on what had happened, because I knew she'd be biting her nails until I called. I tackled my homework next and finished it just before the ten o'clock news began.

The attempted attack on my father wasn't the lead story. There were some problems in the Mideast, and a plane crash in Peru, and other world news items before the TV station got into the story about the political reception and the man who caused the commotion in the ballroom of the Hotel Adolphus.

I could hear the man shout something about oil companies ruining the land, but the camera wasn't close enough for me to see his face.

One of the station's reporters appeared on camera, red, white, and blue balloons and streamers and a noisy crowd behind her, and began telling us what we'd just seen.

The camera finally zeroed in on the three candidates in Dad's party. We heard one or two sentences from Edna Poole about her plan for new laws on drug abuse, before the cameras focused on Stanley Barker, who had an idea about developing Texas ports; but when it was Dad's turn to be televised, we didn't hear what he was saying. The reporter kept going on about how Dad had been attacked by a man who was upset about what was happening to the ecology. I didn't want to hear that again. I wanted to hear what Dad had to tell people about his campaign.

But the coverage of the political reception was over. The station went into a soft drink commercial, then into a political pitch for Governor Jimmy Milco, in which a man with a crown sat with his back to the camera. People scurried around with frightened faces, bowing and scraping, while a deep, authoritative voice asked, "Does Texas need a king? A man who's interested only in power and wealth—wealth his oil company squeezes out of the people? Or do we want to keep a real governor—a man who cares? Governor Jimmy Milco?" As the commercial switched to Milco's gap-toothed grin and heavy jowls, I muttered, "Jerk!" and snapped off the television set.

This had to be the commercial Sally Jo had asked me about. Of course it made me angry, but for more than the commercial itself. It was that *king* idea again. What was this—some sort of conspiracy between the newspaper cartoonist and Milco's campaign office? It was too coincidental that they both had come up with the same weird idea at the same time, because Dad had never acted like a king. He ran a successful independent company, and there was a certain amount of power that went with that. But he wasn't power crazy, and he had a lot of loyal employees. Sure, Dad makes a lot of money, but the way we live is just comfortable, not overdone. Dad thinking he's a king? What if people believed that stupid commercial?

I sighed as I realized that some of them, who didn't know better, probably would.

When Mom and Dad came home I could hear excitement and happiness in their voices. Mom hugged me with delight. "Your father was terrific! I'm so proud of him! You should have seen how well his speech was received!"

"I saw the news on television," I said. "They showed the man who was coming after you. Weren't you scared, Dad?"

He shook his head. "There was a large group around me at the time, and I didn't even see him. The entire episode was over within two or three minutes. It was a minor incident."

"They made a big thing of it on television," I said, "and I hated seeing it happen to you."

Mom's voice was deliberately bright. "Let's not talk about that. Tell us about your father's speech," she said. "I hope they broadcast the part in which Charles questioned how state construction jobs are awarded."

Their expressions were so eager it hurt too much to answer. All I could do was shake my head.

Both Dad and Mom looked puzzled. "What part of the speech did they televise?" Mom asked.

"None of it," I said. "They showed the other candidates first, and we heard just a sentence or two of their speeches. But when Dad was talking we didn't hear what he said. The reporter just told us all over again about the man who tried to attack Dad."

Mom bit her lip, and her eyes snapped with fury. "So much for equal time!"

Dad patted her shoulder and said, "The newspapers will run something about the speech."

"But this would have been free television publicity, and they didn't quote you at all!"

Dad smiled. "You're beginning to sound like Delia."

Mom had to laugh, in spite of her anger. "I can't help it. I take this all very personally."

"You can't," he said. "There are a lot of wild punches thrown in politics, and you have to learn to roll with them."

Mom simmered down, but Dad hadn't convinced me. I didn't want to roll with somebody's punch. I'd rather hit back.

* * *

While we ate breakfast the next morning, Mom, Dad, and I went through one of the local morning newspapers. There was coverage of the reception, but the story was mostly about the disturbance, as though that was more important than anything Dad had said.

"Politics! Yuck!" I muttered and flung my section of the newspaper on the floor. "Why do you want to go through all this, Dad?"

"Someone once said, 'The first requirement of an administrator is that he prove trustworthy.' I agree, and I want to give our state an honest leadership."

"Is it really worth it?"

Dad gave me a long, searching look. "I hope you can answer that question yourself, Cary."

Mom held out a clipping from last evening's *Gazette* and smiled at me. "Your friend, Sally Jo, wrote a pretty good story about you, Cary. Congratulations on giving a fine interview."

Dad smiled, too, and I could see the pride in his eyes. "You have more political know-how than I would have guessed."

I wasn't sure what they meant until I read the story. I came across as a nice clean-cut kid who was proud of her father. Sally Jo had quoted all the things I'd said to describe Dad, and she'd left out my caustic comments about politics. Actually reading in print the things I'd said gave me a peculiar feeling, and I was relieved that the article didn't include what I'd mouthed off about.

The photograph of me was awful, though. She'd caught me while I was saying something, so there I was with my mouth open like a fish gasping for air.

Dad kissed us good-bye and said he was off to Wichita Falls where he was going to speak to the Chamber of Commerce.

"Good luck," Mom said and gave him a big smile. She poured herself another cup of coffee.

When Dad left the dining room I leaned my elbows on the table and looked at Mom. "Tell me the truth," I said. "How do you really feel about Dad's running for governor?"

"We talked it over before Charles made his decision," she said, but her glance slid away from mine.

"Mom," I said, "Sally Jo reminded me that if Dad won, you'd have to give up your law practice, and I'd be in a new school in Austin without my friends."

"I don't know why she was being so negative," Mom said. If your father becomes governor your life will be exciting. You'll meet interesting people and—"

I interrupted. "Mom, she just wanted my reaction. She wasn't trying to cause trouble. But she did make me think . . . not just about me, but about you, too. Won't it bother you to give up your practice?"

"I won't give it up," Mom said. "I'll be able to take a leave of absence from the firm." She tried to smile, but her air of confidence didn't fool me for a minute.

"You'd be away from the courtroom for what—four years? Eight, if Dad's reelected? And what about your work with the rape crisis center? I know that means a lot to you. Wouldn't giving that up be hard to take?"

"Oh, Cary," Mom said, and she reached across the table and took my hands, holding them tightly. "Your father and I are a team, and this isn't the first time we've had to decide what was best for both of us. In this case running for office means so much to your father that it was my own decision to support him in what he wanted to do. I hope you can understand."

"I'd be leaving Allie and Justin—and all my friends."

Mom didn't say anything. She just kept her eyes on mine, waiting patiently until I finally said, "Okay. I understand."

She smiled and squeezed my fingers before she released them. "Good for you, Cary," she murmured.

I wasn't going to give in too graciously, so I added, "But I didn't say I'd like everything about it."

"Me, either," Mom said. She rolled her eyes, and we both laughed. "Come on," she told me. "It's time to take you to school."

When I arrived at school I found that Allie had tacked the article and picture up inside her locker at school, and Justin told me he'd put his copy on the bulletin board in his bedroom. A few of the kids in my class told me they liked the article, a couple teased me about the photograph, but a girl who I thought was a friend made a sarcastic comment about people who think they're famous and turned her back on me.

Why? Just because my father was running for governor I was supposed to let it all go to my head? I pretended that I hadn't heard her, but it hurt.

A new Charles Amberson joke was going around school, too, and a lot of people snickered about it, throwing quick glances at me to see how I'd react, but I didn't. I wouldn't give them the satisfaction.

It was a sunny day, not too hot, so I chose to study on

one of the outside benches, instead of in the library, during my free period, which comes last in the day. I was busy highlighting stuff in my English lit book when Mark suddenly sat down next to me and said, "You were wrong about somebody taking my film as a joke and bringing it back. They didn't."

"I'm sorry," I told him.

He wouldn't give up. "So who took it?"

"How should I know?"

"It all comes down to the fact that you're the only one who didn't want your picture taken." His lower lip curled out in a pout.

"I told you, Mark, I didn't take your film, and I have no idea who did. Are you sure you even had film in your camera?"

"Of course I'm sure!"

This set him off, and I couldn't stand it. "We're supposed to be studying," I said. "Okay? So leave me alone!" I jumped up, grabbed my book, and walked away as fast as I could, but a picture popped into my mind. It was the terrace door at the country club and the man who stood there—Mr. Cragmore. Mark had left his camera on the table by the door. Could Mr. Cragmore have taken the film?

I remembered Mark snapping a photo of me as I stood at the curve in the terrace. I'd heard the men's footsteps approaching before Mark had called out and taken the picture. Were the men in the shot, too? Had they thought they were and been afraid to take the chance? It didn't make sense, but neither did the fact that Mark's film just disappeared out of his camera.

Joan Lowery Nixon

I kept walking in the same direction, trying unsuc-
cessfully to figure out an answer, until I reached the
parking lot. I was turning, ready to go back to my study
bench again, when I noticed an old, dark blue sedan
pull out from where it had been parked at the far side of
the lot. The window on the passenger side was down,
and I caught a quick glimpse of the person inside the
car—a broad-shouldered man with light brown hair.

The car came directly toward me, the afternoon sun-
light blurring the windshield.

I don't know what might have happened. I was too
startled to run or even think. But just then Coach Mac
and some of the senior guys came out of the nearest
building and headed toward one of the school vans,
which was parked in the lot.

The blue sedan turned to the left and drove out the
exit, as though that's what the driver had in mind all
along.

Well, why not? What was the matter with me? I told
myself that I couldn't let my imagination go crazy and
get scared by every little thing. Forget it. I had an
assignment in English lit to finish. I went back to the
bench and forced myself to concentrate on my work.

The first thing I did when Justin and I got to Dad's
campaign office that afternoon was ask Delia if she
knew Francine's last name.

"Of course," she said. "It's *Smith.*"

Francine Smith? There went my imagination again.
The name *Smith* didn't have to be fake. A lot of people

100

are named Smith. "Did Dad tell you about . . . ?" I began.

"Nothing was missing," Delia interrupted. "I don't know what the silly girl thought she was doing!" She picked up a heavy stack of papers and shoved them into my hands. "Could you sort these for me, Cary? For some reason they weren't collated."

I was beginning to know some of the regular volunteers, even though we didn't have much time to talk to each other. I was curious about the people who volunteered. I found out that Mrs. Lane supported herself by selling real estate but felt so strongly about the need for a change of administration that she was donating time every afternoon to Dad's campaign.

Another woman, who often shared my chores, was a retired schoolteacher. A couple of women held office in Dad's political party; there were some grandmothers, some young women with kids in school, and even a few businessmen. Some came every day; some just showed up once in a while.

I tried to talk to Mr. Sibley twice because I was especially curious about him, but he didn't have much to say to me or to anyone else. Once I asked him how long he'd lived in Dallas, and for an instant he stood motionless, staring at me as though he were a terrified rabbit. Then he seemed to pull himself together and hurried off without answering.

I didn't expect Justin to come to the office much longer, especially after Delia lost her temper and blamed him for losing an entire mailing.

"The letters were in those boxes you took to the post office," she said.

"I didn't take any boxes or anything else to the post office," Justin complained.

Delia jabbed a finger at a paper on a clipboard. "Right here is your name with a checkmark beside it," she insisted. "Someone wrote it in and checked you out as you loaded the boxes."

"It wasn't me. Honest."

She sighed and apologized conditionally, rolling her eyes when she said, *"if* there has been a mistake," but she made a couple of strong comments about how important the letter had been and how expensive it was going to be to have it printed all over again.

I'd probably have to fold all those letters. I wasn't looking forward to that, so grumpily I asked Justin, "How could you lose a couple of boxes of mail?"

"I didn't," Justin told me. "Somebody else did. I've been running a lot of errands, but I haven't taken *anything* to the post office. Doesn't anybody believe me?"

I believed him. There were so many people trying to do so many things, it was easy to see how a mistake could have been made. That wasn't the only mistake. Stuff kept getting mislaid, somebody got one of Dad's timetables scrambled in the computer, and a can of cola was spilled over a stack of posters, ruining all of them.

On the way home Justin and I talked about the Halloween dance, which was much more interesting than talking about all the grunt work we were doing in the campaign office. I had gathered all the parts of my

costume, and I couldn't wait to see how Justin and Allie
and Greg were going to look.

On Saturday, the night of the party, I got dressed in
my roadie outfit, sprayed a wide streak of blue in my
hair, and nearly died laughing when I looked at myself
in the mirror.

Mom cracked up when she saw me. "That's a great
costume," she said. "You look like some of those musi-
cians on MTV."

When Justin arrived to pick me up we all whooped
with laughter. He looked hysterically funny in the
straggly blond wig, but in that tight, torn T-shirt he
looked kind of sexy, too.

I wanted to show off our costumes to Dad, but he was
in his office with his campaign managers and a couple of
state legislators.

"Maybe it would be better if you didn't," Mom said.
"They're discussing the investigation of that construction accident, and Charles asked me to take any telephone messages so they wouldn't be interrupted."

I suppose I should have realized that showing off a
Halloween costume would be unimportant kid stuff. "I
hardly ever get to talk to Dad anymore," I complained.
"I'll be glad when he's through with all this."

"Cary, honey," Mom said, "we're still months away
from the primary election. If Charles wins the party
nomination—and I certainly hope he will—you're going to have to face the fact that your father will be even
busier then than now."

"I know," I said.

I tried to think of something to reassure Mom, but Justin grabbed my arm and swung me toward the door. "Come on," he said. "The dance has already started."

Justin and I stopped by the Richardses' house to pick up Greg and Allie. Allie and Greg looked great, and Allie laughed so hard at Justin and me it made me feel good, like our costumes were really the best.

We parked in the big front lot of Loews Anatole Hotel, across from the Dallas Market Center. A few people stared at us as we entered the hotel, but there were enough kids in costume around so that I didn't feel embarrassed. Once we were in the ballroom our school dance committee had decorated with pumpkins, skeletons, and orange and black streamers, it was lots of fun checking out the other costumes and going into hysterics about some of them.

The music was terrific, there was plenty of food, and it was a great party. But just like before, Mark tagged around after me with that stupid camera. That was one of Mark's problems. He never gave up.

"Want me to dump him in the punch?" Justin asked me the umpteenth time that flash went off in my face.

The suggestion sounded good, but I felt sorry for Mark. "No," I said. "He lost the film he took at his own party. Let him take a few more shots. He'll run out of film soon."

The teachers who were chaperoning had come in costumes, too. Mrs. Bantry, our chemistry teacher, came as the Wicked Witch of the West, which was very brave of her, considering the remarks she had to put up with all evening.

While we were dancing I happened to glance over near the door and saw a girl with long straight black hair. I stopped and said to Justin, "Look over there. Is that Francine?"

Justin turned and asked, "Where?"

"There, by the door." But the person who looked like Francine wasn't in sight. "She's gone," I said.

"It couldn't have been Francine," Justin said. "Why would she show up at our school dance?"

"I suppose she wouldn't," I said, "but the girl I saw looked an awful lot like her. I guess Francine has a double."

"Or it's the lighting or your imagination," Justin said. "Come on. Let's dance."

So we did, and I was sorry when the party was over.

We all climbed into Justin's car, still smiling over all the fun, but soon after Justin drove out of the hotel parking lot onto a side street we passed a police car. The officers looked at us and did a U-turn. The lights on top of their car began to flash, and over their loudspeaker we heard the command to pull over.

"What's with them?" Justin said as he pulled the car to the curb. "I didn't do anything."

One of the police officers came up to the driver's window, while the other stood behind Justin's car.

"What did I do?" Justin asked the officer who bent to look in the open window.

He didn't answer. He just stared hard at each of us in turn, then said, "Slowly, now, get out of the car."

It dawned on Justin what the officer was thinking, and he said, "We're coming back from our school's Halloween dance at the Anatole Hotel. Gormley Academy. We're in costume."

"Out of the car," the officer said firmly, as though he'd heard every excuse ever invented and wasn't buying any of them.

I felt like a fool, suddenly aware of what I must look like with my blue hair and miniskirt and torn T-shirt. I glanced back at the other policeman and saw it was a police*woman* and she was on her car radiophone. Great. They were checking out the car. Who did they think we were?

The officer had us line up, and when his partner joined him she said, "This is the car."

"What's wrong with my car?" Justin asked. His voice cracked. We were all beginning to be scared.

"We got a tip about it," the officer said. "Take a look through the car," he told his partner, and the policewoman bent and crawled in. I could see her sweep her arm under the front and back seats, then open the glove compartment. It was in the glove compartment that she came up with something.

As she climbed out of the car she held up a small, clear plastic packet with a handful of capsules in it. "Looks like designer drugs," she said.

"They're not ours!" I cried out. "We don't do drugs."

"Hands behind your backs," the male officer said. Handcuffs were snapped around our wrists, and we were led to the police car.

"You don't understand!" Allie said. "We're Gormley Academy students, and we've just been at a Halloween dance." She glanced over at me, her eyes lit up, and I knew what she was going to do. "Officer!" she said. "This is Cary Amberson, Charles Amberson's daughter."

I groaned. I couldn't help it. Why couldn't Allie keep her mouth shut?

All I could think of were Mom's words: "Whatever you do, Cary, will reflect on your father."

Chapter 10

Photographers from the TV stations and from the newspapers were at the police station waiting for us to arrive. They didn't bother Justin, Allie, and Greg, but microphones were shoved into my face and questions were hurled at me like sharp stones.

"How long have you been on drugs?"

"Have you ever been arrested on drug charges before this?"

"Are you getting any kind of treatment?"

I couldn't stand it. I screamed at them, "None of us has ever taken drugs! And we're dressed like this because we're in costume! We were at a Halloween party!"

It didn't matter what I said. The reporters pushed and shoved and followed us into the station where a detective dressed in a business suit took charge and ushered us into a small room with nothing in it but a plain wooden table and six straight-backed chairs.

The officer who'd arrested us removed our handcuffs.

My wrists hurt, and I rubbed them as I glared at him. "You didn't have to do that!" I complained.

He just shrugged and said, "Procedure," before he left the room.

His partner remained, standing against the wall near the door to the room.

"Who notified the reporters?" I asked her.

"They listen to the police calls," she said.

"You said that Charles Amberson's daughter had been arrested. You did that just so they'd come."

She didn't say anything, but the disgust in her eyes as she looked at me was answer enough. Didn't she understand? This costume wasn't me!

"There's no good hashing this over." The detective was brusque. "Sit down now, all of you. We've got things to get done." He motioned Justin and Greg to one side of the table, Allie and me to the other. When he took his place at the head of the table his suit coat fell open, and we could see his holster and gun.

"I want my parents," Allie said.

"We'll call your parents—all your parents," the detective said. He pulled a notepad and pen from his pocket and added, "Give me their names and phone numbers."

When he'd written down all the information, he tore the page from the pad and handed it to the policewoman. "Get in touch with them, please," he told her.

As she left the room he turned back to us. "I'm Sergeant Masterson, and I'm on narcotics detail."

"We weren't taking drugs!" Justin said. "Someone

planted those in my car and then called you. It had to be the same person."

Sergeant Masterson held up a hand. "I'm doing the talking now," he said. "We'll bring someone in here soon to take your statements. You were all given the Breathalyzer test on the street, but there are more sophisticated tests which can be given here at the station, and I'd like you to take them."

"What kind of tests?" Allie asked.

"They're tests which can be done on samples of your urine and blood. They show not only the quantity of any drug that's in your body but can even specify what type of drug it is."

"We told you we weren't taking drugs!" I insisted.

"If you want to prove it, take the tests," he said.

Someone knocked on the door, and Sergeant Masterson answered it. He spoke in a low voice to the person in the hallway, then turned back to us. "I'll be back soon," he said. "If you need anything, just knock on the door. The officer outside the door will answer."

Before any of us could say anything he had left the room, shutting the door behind him.

We sat there quietly, each of us in a muddle with our own thoughts. I couldn't begin to guess what they planned to do with us, other than have us take the drug tests the detective had told us about. How long would it take for them to get the results from the test and find out we were innocent? What would happen in the meantime? Would we be fingerprinted? Taken before a judge? Put in jail? I tried to remember all the cop movies I'd seen, but my mind was a blank, and I felt a little sick.

Justin glanced toward the door. "I wonder why he left us alone."

"Maybe the room is bugged," Allie said. "I bet they're all in a little room next to ours with a two-way mirror, watching us and listening to what we say to each other."

"There's no mirror in here," Greg grumbled. "You watch too many movies."

Allie was doing better than I was. At least she could remember the movies.

"I wish I could wash my face," I suddenly blurted out.

Allie looked at me a little shyly. "They took a lot of pictures of you."

"I know."

Allie took one of my hands in hers, and Justin got up from his chair on the other side of the table and stood behind me, his hands massaging my neck and shoulders.

"Don't worry, Cary," he said. "You told the reporters that we were in Halloween costumes."

"I don't think they listened or even cared. I look like a tramp, and I've just been arrested on drug charges. That's their big story, and the pictures make it even better."

"People won't believe it," Allie insisted. "Most of our teachers were chaperons at the party. They'll explain about the costumes."

For an instant I was hopeful, but I realized that any explanations would come too late. The original story would probably be front-page news and on tomorrow's local TV news, but follow-up stories—if there were any —would be small items, buried in the back pages of the newspapers and ignored completely in the television broadcasts.

"I should have known better than to go along with the stupid idea for these stupid costumes," I said.

Justin pulled his hands away from my shoulders. "You liked the idea. Remember?"

I didn't want to remember. "How did the drugs get in your car?" I asked.

"I told you, I don't know," Justin said. "Don't you trust me?"

"You told the detective that someone planted them. Why would anyone do a thing like that?"

"You tell *me!"*

Allie put her hands over her ears. "Stop it!" she shouted. "You're making everything worse!"

The room was suddenly silent.

"I'm sorry," I said quietly, looking at each of them in turn. Allie's lip trembled, and tears puddled in her eyes. Greg had his head down, buried in his arms, and Justin's face was still tight and strained with anger. "I'm really sorry," I repeated. "I shouldn't have said the things I did. It's just that I'm worried that this might hurt Dad's campaign."

Justin grunted in disgust. "Cary, haven't you noticed? We're all sick of hearing about your father's campaign."

"I didn't know . . ." I began. "I didn't mean . . ."

"Oh be quiet, Cary," Allie said and began to cry.

Why couldn't I wake up and discover that this had

been nothing more than a horrible dream? Little kid wishes. I knew that this monster wouldn't just go away.

Our parents arrived almost at the same time. Justin's father was so angry and defensive I was afraid he might have a heart attack. He was even more upset when he found out that Justin's car had been impounded.

I was grateful that Mom and Dad didn't ask questions, and they didn't complain about what had been done.

"You must take the tests," they told me, trusting me completely, so I did.

The others did, too, and afterward I was surprised when we were all allowed to go home.

Before we left the station Mom took me into the ladies' room where I could wash my face and brush out my hair. She wrapped me up in a coat she'd brought along, and we walked out into the central room of the police station to join Dad, who had given a statement to the reporters. As we crossed the room a couple of photographers took pictures of me, but since I was covered up, with my face scrubbed clean, I didn't look nearly as interesting.

Once we were safely inside the car I fell apart and sobbed all over Mom's shoulder. She let me cry, but when I'd reached the point at which nothing was left but dry hiccups she hugged me and said, "Cary, honey, we're so terribly sorry that this had to happen to you."

I struggled to sit upright and stared at Mom. *"You're* sorry? *I'm* the one who's sorry. *I'm* the one who ruined things."

"No," Mom said firmly. "You're not at fault, and neither are your friends. It's the situation . . . the news interest in Charles . . . in our family." Her words faded away.

"Those awful pictures of me will be in the newspapers and on television."

"Maybe not," Dad said. "I gave the reporters the facts and told them how they could check them out."

"Sure," Mom said, and squeezed my shoulders in another hug. "None of you had taken drugs—the tests will prove it—and the story will be nothing more than a false alarm. False alarms don't make news stories."

But Mom and Dad had been too optimistic. On the front page of the local newspapers the next morning were blown-up pictures of me being led into the police station in handcuffs. There was the weird hair, the crazy makeup, the ragged black tights. I looked as though I'd been picked up in some alley. The headline over the photo in one of the newspapers read: CANDIDATE'S DAUGHTER ARRESTED IN DRUG BUST. The photo and headline in the other newspaper were just as bad.

The stories were full of "alleged" and "appeared to be" to keep the newspapers out of trouble legally, and they did briefly mention the Halloween dance; but one of the newspapers—the one with the mean political cartoonist—included a statement Governor Milco had made, when he announced his campaign for reelection, about what should be done with juvenile drug offenders. Anyone who read the stories would probably begin thinking of a few other political candidates whose kids had got into trouble and start clucking and shaking their heads, wondering what this world was coming to.

I got plenty of odd looks while we were at church. Some of them were curious; some were contemptuous. All I could do was pretend I didn't notice, keep my gaze straight ahead, and smile at people I knew, but it was a horrible time to have to live through.

From the moment we got home the family telephone kept ringing, but there were no calls on my private line. I felt miserable about what Justin and I had said to each other and about the way I'd treated Allie and Greg, too.

I called Allie and got a busy signal, so I called Greg, but he was grounded and his dad wouldn't even let him come to the phone. I wanted to call Justin, but I had already apologized. Why couldn't he call me?

After a couple of tries I got through to Allie, and I blurted out, "I was terrible last night. I'm sorry, Allie."

"Hey, it's okay," she said. "We were all scared. I was never so scared in my whole life."

We were interrupted by a clattering noise. "Allie?" I asked.

There was more banging and bumping before she answered. "Sorry," she said. "I dropped the phone."

I smiled to myself. It was comforting that Allie was still the same. "Why don't you come over?" I asked. "Or should we go to a movie?"

"Ohhhh, I can't," Allie wailed. "My aunt and her family are going to be here for dinner, and I have to help watch her little kids. The two-year-old—Timmy— you'd never guess all the stuff he can get into. Last time they were here he started fooling with my parents'

116

clock radio and got everything so mixed up you wouldn't believe it, and . . ."

Allie rattled on. I kept telling myself that she had a perfectly good reason for not being able to come over, and I shouldn't take it so personally, but I was glad when Allie finally interrupted herself with a groan. "They're here," she said. "I've got to go."

I held the phone in my lap and tried to use mental telepathy. Call me, Justin! Call me right this minute!

It didn't work.

Delia had come over, as had Robert, a lawyer, and Dad's campaign managers, and a few other people I'd never met. They shut themselves up with Dad in his office, and that was the last Mom and I saw of him for over two hours. Every now and then the phone would ring, but Dad would answer it.

I was sitting at the kitchen table, munching on what was left of my frozen marshmallow cookies and reading the Sunday comics when Dad came into the kitchen to get a drink of water. I could see the exhaustion in his face.

"The telephone calls are about me, aren't they?" I asked him.

He put down his glass and wrapped an arm around my shoulders. "Honey," he said, "there are a lot of busybodies in this world. We aren't going to pay any attention to them."

"But they won't vote for you."

"We've worked out a statement to give to the media. It will explain everything."

"You've been working on it an awfully long time."

"That's not all we've been doing. There are many aspects to a political campaign." He stretched and rolled his head, trying to ease the tension in his neck. "And to investigations. We've got a private investigator looking for Cragmore's former superintendent, but so far there's no trace of him."

Mom came into the kitchen and smiled when she saw Dad. "Oh, good," she said. "Have they gone?"

His answering smile was wry. "Unfortunately, there's still work to do."

"Would they like coffee?"

"Thanks, but Velma sent a pot of coffee in about half an hour ago."

"Maybe I should feed them. What do you think? Sandwiches?"

"No," Dad said firmly as he walked across the kitchen. "Let them get good and hungry, and maybe they'll leave."

I laughed, and he looked at me with surprise. "That's not a joke," he said. "I mean it."

Dad paused at the door and glanced back at Mom. "Laura," he said, "they told me I appeared stiff on camera, that I needed to . . . 'loosen up and lighten up.' That's the way they put it." He looked embarrassed, and his voice dropped as he said, "Do you think I seem stiff? Do I make a bad appearance?"

Mom ran to Dad, gave him a quick hug, and said, "Of course not, Charles! Don't listen to them."

"They're paid to be my advisers."

"I don't care. Don't try to change your personality to please them. Be yourself."

"They pointed out that many people base their vote strictly on how the candidate comes across on television."

"You come across as a man with intelligence and dignity and honor," Mom insisted, "and my opinion counts, too."

"Thanks," Dad said. He gave her a grateful smile and left the room.

I went upstairs. Maybe I should call Justin and try to make up. Maybe Justin had been trying to call me and couldn't get through. Yes. That had to be it.

As I opened my bedroom door I stopped. Something didn't feel right.

One set of the pale blue curtains that edged the windows hung neatly, but at the far window they'd been drawn together, covering the window. I hadn't left them like that. Someone had been in my room.

I held my breath and looked and listened.

Someone was still there!

Chapter 11

In the mirror that hung over the chest of drawers I could see the door to the walk-in closet. It was open just a crack, and as I waited I thought I saw it move.

I didn't even bother to shut the bedroom door. I just tore down the stairs, yelling at the top of my lungs. I made so much noise that if anyone had tried to follow me I couldn't have heard him.

Everyone in the house came running, and while I tried to explain what had scared me, Dexter broke from the group and took the stairs three at a time.

"We should call the police," Mom said.

But Delia shook her head. "Do we want more bad press? Cary said she didn't see anyone. Just because the curtains were out of place . . ."

Velma interrupted her. "I didn't touch those curtains."

Delia ignored her and asked, "Why don't we wait and see what Dexter finds?"

Dad and a couple of others had already started up the stairs by the time Dexter leaned over the upper railing and beckoned to Dad. "No one's in the house now," Dexter said, and the way he emphasized *now* showed us that he thought someone really had been in my room.

Mom and I looked at each other. I could tell she was as frightened as I was. She and I ran upstairs, the stragglers following.

As we entered my bedroom I caught a glimpse of Dexter tucking something under his white coat, behind his back. He moved so quickly I couldn't tell what it was, but I thought it looked like a gun. What would Dexter be doing with a gun?

Dexter pointed to the far window. He had pulled the curtains wide, and we could see that the window was open. "I'm pretty sure that someone was in this room," he said. "It looks as though he made a quick getaway when Cary began yelling."

Dad poked his head out the window and drew back inside. "He could have climbed up the oak," he said. "I didn't realize the branches came so close to this window." He checked the other window, which was locked, and faced me. "Cary," he said, "if you want a window open, it would be safer to open this one."

"I didn't open either of them," I said. In Dallas we go from air-conditioning to heat to air-conditioning, and there are very few days on which we open windows.

"The glass was cut," Dexter said. He pointed to the top of the sash where there was a neat round hole, about four inches across, directly under the lock.

"Why didn't the security system . . . ?" Mom began. She interrupted herself. "Oh, of course. We only turn it on at night."

"We'll inform the police," Dad said, "and when they've examined everything, we'll get a glazier to come and repair that window."

"This doesn't make any sense," Mom said. "It's daylight, and we have a house filled with people."

Dexter glanced toward Dad, then looked away as though he couldn't meet Dad's eyes. He walked over to where Mom and I were standing and said, "All day either Mr. Amberson or I answered the door. We knew everyone who came into the house."

"There was the man from the gas company," Velma said, "but he didn't ask to go inside the house."

We all looked at her. "This is Sunday. No one from the gas company would be reading meters on a Sunday," Mom said.

"Oh, he wasn't readin' meters," Velma said. "He said there was a gas leak somewhere in the neighborhood, and I wasn't to pay no mind to him. He'd just be checkin' around outside."

Velma didn't have to read our faces. She realized what had happened and groaned. "He was the one who broke in, wasn't he?"

My heart began beating hard again, and I was so scared it was hard to get the question out. "What if the man comes back?"

Dad put his hands on my shoulders and looked into my eyes. "Cary, none of us knows why he was here," Dad said. "It was probably a burglary attempt, and because of that tree against the house, your room was the most accessible."

We all searched to see if anything upstairs had been taken, but nothing was missing.

Dad took charge, leading us downstairs, and in just a few minutes the police arrived. A lab crew went upstairs with the detective—Jim Slater again—but in a short while he came down to the kitchen and talked to Velma. Then he sat on the sofa in the den across from Mom, Dad, and me. He was a large man, and the notepad he opened was almost lost in his hand.

I was curious. "What did Velma say about the man she talked to?"

"She wasn't too specific. She was more aware of the uniform than the person wearing it," Sergeant Slater answered. "She did say she thought he had brown hair, was tall and broad-shouldered, and was probably in his late twenties or early thirties. She agreed to come to headquarters tomorrow morning and go through mug shots."

Sergeant Slater asked a few basic questions, and I answered them.

"In case this break-in was because of you, Cary, you must tell the detective everything. Tell him about the phone calls," Mom said, so I did, and when we got through the questions which he asked about Nora— most of which I didn't have answers for—I told him about Ben Cragmore and the man with the scratchy voice, and what I could remember hearing.

"And you said they were talking about someone named Bill?"

"I think that was the name."

Dad spoke up. "Could it have been Bill Fletcher?"

"They didn't say his last name."

Dad turned to the detective. "I thought of Bill Fletcher because he's on the committee that awards the highway contracts."

"Bill's a pretty common name." Sergeant Slater heaved himself to his feet and said, "We'll check into everything. The person in your house was probably just someone looking for things he could sell to buy drugs. But we won't take any chances. The publicity your family is getting could attract some strange types, so we'll put a watch on your house for a few days."

As Mom and Dad walked with Sergeant Slater to the front door I could hear them talking in low undertones. Things they didn't want to frighten me with, I supposed.

It was only after the detective had left and I was thinking over everything that had happened that I remembered seeing Dexter tuck something under his jacket behind his back. I still thought it might have been a gun.

I managed to get Dad aside, which wasn't easy, and told him what I thought.

Dad just said, "Yes, Dexter has a gun. More than one, I understand. He works out at a sharpshooter range each week."

"A sharpshooter range? Why?"

"Why not?"

"Okay. But our house isn't a sharpshooter range," I

125

said. "Why would Dexter be carrying a gun around here?"

"He was planning to go to the range this evening, and perhaps he was getting his guns ready," Dad said. "I wouldn't be concerned about it, Cary."

"All right," I answered, but I really wasn't satisfied. I was still just a little bit suspicious of Dexter.

Justin didn't call, and I missed him more and more, so after dinner I called him. Justin's mother answered and said only that she'd call him to the phone. She didn't mention what had happened after the dance, but I could feel my face burning, and I had to swallow a couple of times before I could answer Justin when he said hello.

"I thought maybe you'd tried to call and kept getting the busy signal," I babbled. I was miserable because I was talking too loudly and saying stupid things, but there was no way to start over.

"I didn't try to call you," Justin said, and I felt even worse.

"O-oh," I stammered and wished I could think of what to say next.

"I'm kind of busy right now," Justin said.

Why was he being so mean? I wasn't the only one who'd said unkind things last night. "Okay," I said. "If that's the way you want it."

"What is that supposed to mean?"

I took a deep breath and attempted to sound calm. "I just called to apologize again, Justin. I'm sorry I was rude to everybody last night."

"It's okay," he mumbled. "Apology accepted."

There was silence for a few minutes while my temper began to rise. Finally I said, "That's it?"

"Well, sure. What am I supposed to say?"

"I wasn't the only one who was rude. How about what you said to me?"

"I wasn't being rude. I was just telling you the truth."

"You hurt my feelings."

"I can't help that."

I was so hurt I wanted to cry, but I tried to stay cool and explain. "Look, Justin, this has been very hard on me."

"On *all* of us, Cary," he said quickly.

"All right, then. On all of us. I hoped you'd understand. I hoped you'd want to make up."

For just an instant his voice softened. "We don't have to make up. Everything's okay, Cary."

"Are you sure?"

"Of course I'm sure."

"Do you want to come over?"

The edge crept back into his voice. "Tonight? I'm sorry, Cary. I can't. I left my homework to the last minute."

"I've still got some stuff to do for English. We could do our homework together."

"We've tried that. It doesn't always get done."

I gulped and said, "I miss you, Justin."

"Yeah," he said, and I could hear the embarrassment in his voice. "Well, look, I'll see you at school tomorrow. Okay?"

"Okay," I said and slowly hung up the phone, so miserable I felt sick to my stomach.

Joan Lowery Nixon

Somehow I was able to finish my homework, and somehow I was able to make it through school the next day, in spite of the political cartoon that appeared in one of the morning newspapers. It showed Dad, again with a crown on his head, looking pompous as he was giving a speech. In a balloon coming out of his mouth were the words, "We need to emphasize the *quality* of education." Behind Dad was a girl who was supposed to be me, dressed like trash and leaning against a long low car that was more like the Batmobile than Justin's car.

Mom squeezed my shoulder and said, "Don't let it bother you, Cary."

"That drawing's gross, and I'm not like that," I mumbled.

"Everyone knows that," Mom said.

"No they don't. People who don't know me will think I'm awful."

"Oh, Cary . . . I don't know what I can say that will help."

It wasn't Mom's fault. Why take my bad mood out on her? "I'll get over it," I said, and managed to choke down some cereal.

A little while later Mom drove me to school. When I stalled about getting out of the car Mom said, "Honey, you'll find that your friends are on your side. They'll make it easier for you."

"It's not that," I said. "I keep thinking about someone being in my room. I'm afraid he'll come back."

"He won't, and you can't keep worrying about it." Mom used her firm tone that probably made juries think twice. I know I always paid attention when I heard it. "The police will take care of things," she insisted. "And there will always be someone around to keep an eye on you."

"Okay, Mom," I interrupted and gave her a quick kiss good-bye. Cars were lining up behind us, and this was not the place for a long discussion. I hopped out of the car and avoided some of the clusters of kids outside as I made my way into the main building.

Of course, someone had tacked the cartoon on the main bulletin board in the front hall, and it remained there until somebody in the attendance office spotted it and tore it down. It was harder to take the embarrassed glances that slid away from mine and the hostility I got from a few of the kids than it was to take the teasing. In a way I welcomed the teasing. It laid everything out in the open so we could make fun of it. The shared laughter was a way of saying that everything was going to be all right.

During lunch period Allie jumped in with enthusiasm. "If you think Cary looked bad, you should have seen *me!* I looked so tough even the Hell's Angels would have been afraid of me."

"Yeah? I didn't see any pictures of *you* in the newspapers," someone said.

"Oh, the photographers *desperately* wanted my picture, but each time they tried to take it their lenses cracked." Allie tried to strike a glamour pose but lost her balance and fell off the bench.

Even Greg—who had slunk into class with dark circles under his eyes, looking as though he hadn't slept the entire weekend—joined in the laughter.

Joan Lowery Nixon

Allie kept hamming it up, all for my benefit. I wished Justin was with us to hear Allie's jokes, but Justin had spent the day avoiding me, and there wasn't anything I could do about it. I'd apologized the night before, I'd told him I'd like to see him, and now whatever happened between us was up to him.

I didn't want to face the idea that there might never be anything between us again, because that thought hurt too much. Justin would come around. I had to make myself believe that he would.

Dexter picked me up in Mom's Cadillac, and as I climbed into the car, I caught a glimpse of Justin's white BMW leaving the parking lot. Someone was with him. Cindy Parker. She thought nothing of borrowing my money, my books, and even my makeup. Did she think she could borrow Justin, too? I felt a terrible pang of sick jealousy that hit like a rock thumping into my chest.

Forget Justin. He was history. That's the way he wanted it—the way we *both* wanted it.

No, it wasn't. I had really cared about Justin. I missed him, and it hurt.

I was glad that Dexter didn't want to talk, because I didn't feel like talking to anyone. When we got home and I found out that no one needed that car the rest of the day I decided to drive myself to Dad's campaign office.

"I think your Mama wants someone to go with you," Velma said. "Better get Dexter to take you."

I didn't want to go with Dexter. I still felt uncomfortable with him—maybe even a little suspicious. Dad's explanation hadn't helped a bit. "I'll be all right, Velma," I insisted. "I don't like being watched over every minute." I couldn't help smiling at the brave way I sounded. "At least while it's daylight," I added.

She didn't think it was funny. "I don't know about that. Let me go ask Dexter."

I took the car keys from the shelf and picked up my shoulder bag. "There's not enough time. I've got to go now. I'll be home for dinner." I was out the door before she had time to answer.

I wondered why I'd even come when I walked into the office. I got some of the same sly turn-away looks that I'd had to put up with at school, and a few people stared rudely, as though their X-ray vision could penetrate my conservative shirt and skirt and discover the wild heavy-metal outfit that must be hidden beneath them.

Delia, in her customary frantic rush, managed to greet me and shoo me off to my usual table. She plopped a large box of colored brochures next to me. "Label them all," she said and waved toward more boxes piled against the wall. "There are thousands and *thousands* to get done. This is an important statewide mailing."

"Where are the labels?" I asked.

"On the table," Mrs. Lane said, shoving another box toward me. She studied me with disapproval and sniffed as I sat down.

I picked up the slick-paper brochure on top of the stack in the box and saw the full-color family photo Mom, Dad, and I had posed for a couple of months ago.

Joan Lowery Nixon

It was the all-dressed-up kind of photo we sent to friends at Christmas. We were smiling happily, totally ignorant that it wasn't just Dad who'd be campaigning. It would be Mom and me, too.

What would the voters think who saw this picture and read the brochure about Dad's ideas and plans? I tried to put myself in their place.

> _Want a governor who'll give you a good honest government? Forget it. Who's interested in something as boring as campaign issues? No, we want to base our votes on how much money the candidate has got, what we think of his wife's hairdo and the estimated price of the clothes she's wearing, and what his daughter is up to. My, my, the daughter looks like such a nice, wholesome teenager in this photo, but do you want to know the truth? She's wild. She runs around with drug users. Of course I know what I'm talking about. I saw it on TV, didn't I?_

Delia swept past, pulling the brochure from my hands and slapping it onto the table. "Cary, dear," she said, "you can read it later. We are running way, way, _way_ behind schedule, and these have to get out."

Obediently I joined Mrs. Lane in slapping printed peel-off labels on the folded brochures and piling them into another box. I wondered when I'd graduate—if ever—to a more interesting job. I had to remind myself that it didn't matter. Whatever needed to be done to get Dad his party's nomination, that's what I'd do.

132

Mr. Sibley came from the hallway, struggling to carry a heavy box. He staggered to where I was sitting and dropped his box on the floor next to my chair. A button was missing from his same old vest, and I wondered if the heavy box could have torn it off. But there were more important things than missing buttons on my mind.

Before he could get away I put a hand on his arm to detain him and asked, "Mr. Sibley, you've been working almost every day for my father's campaign. I'm taking a kind of poll, just for my own interest, asking volunteers why they're giving up their own time to work on my father's campaign."

Mr. Sibley shrugged and tried to pull away. I could feel his arm trembling, and it surprised me so much that I let go, but I didn't take my eyes off his face.

"I-I didn't have the chance to get involved in politics when I was young," he said. "Now I'm making up for lost time."

"Are you retired?" I asked, but he scurried out of earshot.

Why didn't he want to talk to me? I remembered that Mr. Sibley had come to work as a volunteer the day after Mark's party. Had he been sent here to spy on me?

Mr. Sibley? No. I couldn't let my imagination go crazy.

"How's it going? Another exciting job?"

I looked up to see Sally Jo Wilson. "Hi," I said. "Thanks for the story you wrote about me. It was a good one."

Sally Jo's face crinkled with one of her flashing smiles,

but beyond her I could see Delia advancing at a fast pace.

Then and there I got an idea. I didn't know if it would work. It might be the worst and dumbest idea I'd ever had, but there was only one way to find out.

I leaned close to Sally Jo. "Listen," I said. "Can we get together somewhere? I need to talk to you."

Chapter 12

I called home and told Velma I'd be a little late for dinner. She began to argue—as I knew she would—that I was supposed to come straight home, but I quickly said, "Gotta go. I'll see you later," and hung up.

As soon as Delia closed the campaign office at five o'clock, I drove to the small Italian café where Sally Jo had said she'd meet me. The restaurant was in an old house in a small, formerly residential neighborhood, in which art galleries, photographers, and small shops lined the streets. The lawns were neatly mowed and flowers bloomed around the concrete pillars that decorated the wide front porches. This was far from my own neighborhood so I wasn't likely to meet anyone I knew here. I was sure that's why Sally Jo had picked it.

Sally Jo had not arrived when I stepped into the tiny, dimly lit entry. I glanced at my watch. I was five minutes early.

"Do you want me to show you to a table?" a short, pudgy Italian man asked me, but I shook my head. I felt more secure in the small, dark room.

"I'll just wait here," I told him.

I leaned against the wall. From where I stood I could see into the dining room, which was filled with square tables covered with red-and-white checked gingham tablecloths, each table decorated with one stubby candle flickering through a red glass hurricane lamp. Fortunately, there were other and better lights in the room.

Only two tables were taken. A pair of elderly men were bent almost into their soup bowls, slowly and steadily slurping soup into their mouths, and a man and a woman were eating silently, as though they were bored with each other.

When Sally Jo arrived, we were seated; she ordered a house salad, ziti, and garlic bread. I wanted nothing but iced tea, to the obvious disappointment of our waiter. When it came I sipped at it, but Sally Jo tore into her food as though she were in a contest to see how fast she could make it disappear.

"I'll eat, you talk," she said. "What have you got on your mind?"

I wasn't sure how to get into it or how much I wanted to tell her, so I answered with another question. "You told me that reporters know how to find out almost anything about anyone. How do you do it?"

One of her eyebrows went up and down like a window shade. "Depends on what you want to find out." She wiped runny garlic butter off her fingers and waited for what I'd say next.

"Let's say that I—I want to find out about a person."

"Find out what?"

"Everything."

Her eyebrows finally settled into place, and she said, "I'm not sure just what you mean. Do you want information about his hometown, background, past and present addresses, that sort of thing?"

"I guess," I said. "Like all those things you knew about me."

"You'll find a lot of information in the main library and in the courthouse," she said. "There's a crisscross directory in the library which lists addresses and who lives in each building. The libraries also carry professional journals which usually tell where their members went to school, the names of their spouses, their hometowns, and maybe other pieces of information about their lives. A lot of them have pictures, too, and that often helps."

Sally Jo continued. "If a person has recently moved, and you need to find his current address, for a small fee the post office will give it to you.

"In the courthouse you can find records of birth, marriage, divorces, financial assets, and even if the person was involved in any bankruptcies, civil suits, or had any criminal charges filed against him." She paused and searched my face. "Am I giving you the answers you want?"

"In a way." Before she could answer I asked, "What if you don't know someone's name?"

"Do you know what this person looks like?"

"Yes."

"Is there some way of tying him to someone else or to

Joan Lowery Nixon

a profession? You haven't given me enough information."

I leaned forward. "You know so much about finding out information about people. I need you to help me."

As Sally Jo polished off every scrap of lettuce on her salad plate, her smile flickered more brightly than the candle between us. "I'll be glad to help you," she said, "but I'll need your reason for wanting to know about the person."

The waiter took away Sally Jo's salad plate and put down a huge plate of ziti. It did look good, and my stomach growled with hunger. I had to remind myself that I was expected home for dinner very soon.

"May I please have more garlic bread?" Sally Jo asked the waiter, and she poured a thick layer of Parmesan cheese over the sauce on her ziti.

"It can't get into the newspaper," I told her.

"I said I'd help you. I'm not interviewing you for a story."

I needed Sally Jo's help. I had to trust her. Carefully, I glanced to both sides. Another couple had come into the restaurant, but they were seated on the opposite side of the room. No one was close enough to hear us, but I lowered my voice anyway and told her what little I remembered about the conversation I'd overheard, the phone calls from the woman named Nora, and the break-in at our house.

"Dad says that every candidate, every celebrity, every person who gets even a little bit famous has to deal with a few weird people."

"He's right," Sally Jo said. She finished chewing a

138

mouthful of ziti and added, "Your father has talked to the police, though, hasn't he?"

"Yes," I said. "But I'm not sure what the police really think. The last detective said he thought the break-in was a simple burglary.

Sally Jo pushed her half-eaten plate of ziti aside, and her eyes were intense as she leaned toward me. "What do you think, Cary?"

"I think Nora was trying to warn me. We shouldn't have changed my telephone number. Now, I'll never find out what she wanted to tell me."

"Can you figure out what she might have wanted to warn you about?"

I shook my head. "She didn't tell me enough. But there's only one thing it could be tied to. I'm pretty sure that those men I heard on the country club terrace said something they don't want anyone to know, and they think I overheard it, because the phone calls, my being followed—all that stuff began after the night of Mark's party."

"Let's go over what you heard," Sally Jo said.

"I told you. I didn't pay that much attention. It didn't make much sense to me."

"Have you tried hard to remember it?"

"No. I guess not."

"Is there some reason why you're afraid to remember? Do you think you might be mentally blocking the conversation?"

"No," I said again. "It didn't frighten me. I was more concerned about them thinking I was a snoop."

"All right, then," Sally Jo said. "Let's see how much

you can remember now. Lean back in your chair. Take three long, deep breaths. Relax."

I tried to do as she said, but she chuckled. "No, no, no. Don't grip the arms of the chair. Rest your hands in your lap, palms up. Start with your toes. Consciously relax every inch of your body. Here . . . do as I tell you."

Her voice became low and soft and monotonous as she recited a ritual about relaxing, beginning with my feet and working up to my shoulders. "Your neck is heavy. Let it relax. That's it. The muscles of your face are heavy. Your eyelids close; your chin drops. Let the muscles in your cheeks sag and relax."

She was quiet for a few moments, and by this time I was almost asleep. Softly, she said, "Cary, stay in your relaxed position and tell me what you were wearing on the terrace. Picture the setting and describe everything you can. Then tell me about running away from Mark."

The memory came back to me with such clarity that I could even smell the fragrances in the warm night air. I described all that I could and even told her how I felt hiding in the dark corner of the terrace.

"You heard two men speaking," Sally Jo said. "What did they say?"

For an instant I began to tense, but I took another deep breath and concentrated on relaxing until I could almost hear their voices. "A man with a strange, rough voice said that a problem had been taken care of and they were back in the ball game—if things didn't

140

change—and I think he told the other man not to worry."

"What about the other man? What was his part of the conversation?"

"I'm pretty sure the second man was Ben Cragmore. He was talking about some man they knew who was causing the problem. Mr. Cragmore was surprised this man would do something."

"Did he say what it was the man did?"

"No."

"Did he mention any names?"

I tried so hard to pull the name from my memory that I began gripping my hands together.

"Relax," Sally Jo told me, and I tried, but I couldn't.

I opened my eyes and looked at her. "The name didn't mean anything to me at the time," I said. "I think it was *Bill*. But it could have been something that rhymed with *Bill*, like *Phil*. Or maybe *Gil*."

"Anything else about this man?"

"Yes." I could hear the words plainly in my mind. "The guy with the scratchy voice said, 'Because of his big mouth he's up a creek.'"

I saw that Sally Jo had taken out her notebook and had been writing. As she made another notation I asked, "Did you hypnotize me?"

She grinned. "No. I just helped you relax. I go through that routine myself whenever I'm under a lot of stress. It's as good as a nap, and it helps me think better."

"I wish I could have remembered the name he said."

"You may remember it later. At least we've got something to go on." She wrote down something else and said, "We can start with Ben Cragmore. Since he's president of a large construction firm, there should be a lot of available information about him."

"What about the man with Mr. Cragmore?" I asked.

"All you know about him is what he looks like and that he has a distinctive voice."

"Rough, scratchy," I repeated. "Very strange."

"I'll ask around," she told me. "You never know what somebody might come up with."

There were a couple of other people I wondered about, and Sally Jo might help me with one of them.

"I think we should find out as much as we can about Dexter Kline," I said.

"Who's Dexter Kline?"

"I guess you'd call him our butler, but he does what's needed around the house and chauffeurs when it's necessary, and he started working for us just two months ago. Of course, Velma knows the schedules too—Velma Hansel—but I trust her. She's been our housekeeper for years."

"You trust her but not Dexter. Any reason except that he's only worked for you for a short time?"

"I haven't got any real reason," I said and blushed because I knew she'd think I was stupid. "It's just—a feeling. I don't know."

Sally Jo nodded. She had me spell Dexter's name and made a notation in her notebook. "Where's Dexter Kline from?"

"Dallas, I guess. Mom and Dad hired him through an employment agency." I gave her the agency's name.

"I know the agency. It's a reputable one," she said.

Sally Jo looked at me so intently that I was suddenly frightened. Why was I telling her all this? She was a reporter, and how could I be sure she'd keep her promise not to use the information?

It was as if she were reading my mind, because she suddenly said, "What you told me is confidential—just between us—but if and when we get close to the answers, if they add up to anything, then I'll have first crack at writing the story. Do you agree?"

That was only fair. "Yes," I answered.

Sally Jo smiled, pulled her plate toward her, and picked up her fork. "Want some delicious, cold ziti?" she asked.

I pushed back my chair and stood. "No, thanks," I told her. "I'm already late for dinner." I started to take out my wallet, but—her mouth full—she waved it away. "Our dinner will be paid for by the *Gazette,*" she told me.

"Thanks for helping me," I said.

"Glad to. And when I get the information you wanted I'll get in touch with you."

As I left the restaurant and walked to the car I wondered if I'd made a big mistake. I'd told the police everything, and they were already investigating. What made me think a reporter could come up with information the police couldn't find?

What if neither of them could find the answers in time?

From what Nora had told me, I was a target, and I needed all the help I could get.

Chapter 13

As I fished through my shoulder bag, looking for my car keys, my fingers touched the extra key to the campaign office, and I realized I still hadn't remembered to give it back.

I was glad I hadn't. Now I could use it.

I hadn't told Sally Jo about Edwin Sibley, because my suspicions were too vague, but there was something about Mr. Sibley that made me very uncomfortable. I could get the information about him all by myself. I didn't need Sally Jo's help with this.

A few minutes later I parked in front of campaign headquarters. All the lights were on, as they had been ever since the night Francine had gone through the things in Delia's office, so I had a clear view of most of the interior. I reminded myself that anyone passing by would easily be able to see what I was up to.

I quickly unlocked the front door, locked it again, and strode down the hallway to Delia's office.

Her desk was orderly, with tidy stacks of papers in

two in- and out-boxes. Good. That would make my search much easier.

That's what I thought, but I was wrong. Frantically, I replaced each stack of paper and went on to the next. It had to be here, and I had to find it soon. I didn't have that much time to spare. Where was the list of volunteers? I couldn't find it!

Finally, I began searching through the drawers in Delia's desk, and there it was in a folder in the right-hand bottom drawer: a complete alphabetized list of names, addresses, and telephone numbers for all the volunteers.

I copied the information about Mr. Edwin Sibley. His address was on Puckett Street. I hadn't heard of Puckett Street, but there was a street map in Mom's car, and I could look it up there.

I ran out of the office, locking it tightly after I reminded myself *not* to turn out the lights. The night air was comfortably cool with a light breeze, the forerunner of a cold front that was moving down and would bring with it rain and a drop in temperature to the sixties.

When I got into my car I spread out the map and found Puckett Street without any trouble. Surprisingly, it was a short street near the downtown area.

As I turned on the ignition and swung out on Commerce, I was nervous. The palms of my hands were wet against the leather cover on the steering wheel. What was I going to do when I got to Mr. Sibley's address? So far, I had no idea.

I almost gave up and drove home, but I'd come this

far; at least I could see where Mr. Sibley lived. The shy little man who always wore the same clothes—maybe seeing his house or apartment would give me a better idea of who he was and why he had volunteered to help Dad.

I drove down Puckett Street, searching in vain for Mr. Sibley's address. On the second try I drove more slowly, passing old storefronts, some of them vacant, a small building with broken opaque windowpanes that must have once contained some kind of factory, and a bar whose name was spelled out in a sickly green neon. I pulled to the side and read the address again: 145 Puckett. I could barely make out the faded numbers on the side of one of the vacant stores. Its windows were broken out, and the area around it was decorated with knee-high weeds, empty cans, and broken bottles.

Either someone had made a mistake, or Mr. Sibley had lied and given a fake address.

Each of the listings of the volunteer workers included a telephone number. Had Mr. Sibley given a wrong telephone number, too? There was an easy way to find out.

The door of the bar opened, and yellow light spilled in a broad splash across the pavement. A man lurched out of the bar, the door closed, and the brightness disappeared, but there was enough light from the street lamps for me to see him lift his head, take a look at me, and stumble in my direction. I floored the accelerator as I swung into the center of the street and raced out of that neighborhood.

I found I was in big trouble when I arrived home.

Mom and Dad were furious. I might have got away with driving myself to the campaign office, but they were really mad about my staying so late.

"But I called Velma," I said. "I told her I'd be late for dinner. I went out for a few minutes with Sally Jo."

"After what has happened . . ." my father began.

"Do you have any idea how worried we were?" Mom said at the same time.

"I didn't mean . . ."

Those were the last words I said for a long time. Dad calls it "laying down the law," and I suppose I deserved it. The final announcement was that I was not to go anywhere by myself, day or night, until I was given permission.

"Do you understand?" Dad asked.

"Yes," I said, "and I'm sorry I scared everybody. I really am."

We ate a late dinner. That was my fault, too. At first, Mom and Dad didn't talk much, but then Dad told Mom a little about how the investigation into the construction accident was going. "The steel beams they used were not the size listed in the original specifications," Dad said. "However, Ben Cragmore claims he'd ordered the proper size, and the company supplying the steel had made the mistake. His superintendent had gone ahead with it, making variations, in order to keep the project on schedule. Of course, Cragmore proved his good intentions by firing the superintendent."

"What about the other superintendent—the one the

worker had told you about? Herb something. Herb Gill-
man?"

"Herb *Gillian,*" Dad said. "According to the private
investigator I hired, there's evidence that Mr. Gillian
moved to the San Francisco area. We have the moving
company's records showing the furniture was put in
storage. The address to which the furniture was supposed to have been sent doesn't exist."

I felt creepy. This was too much like Mr. Sibley. His
address didn't exist either.

Something else occurred to me. "Did Velma look at
mug shots today?" I asked.

"Yes," Mom said, "and she complained about how
much time it took. She was disappointed that she wasn't
able to recognize our burglar in any of the photos."

I was disappointed, too. I wanted the police to catch
him and find out what he was doing in our house. No
matter what Mom and Dad said, I didn't believe the
man was a burglar. I hated to face the idea that he had
come because of me!

Velma had done her usual best with dinner, but I
couldn't eat. When I was finally excused, I went upstairs
to do homework. I was keeping up my grades, just as I'd
promised Mom, but it was ruining my social life. I didn't
have time for long phone conversations with Allie.

But before I opened my notebook, there was one
quick thing I needed to do. I dialed Mr. Sibley's telephone number.

When a male voice answered, I asked for Mr. Sibley,
and winced as the person called him to the telephone
by yelling his name at the top of his lungs.

Joan Lowery Nixon

The address was a fake, but the telephone number was right, and that surprised me.

When Mr. Sibley answered I identified myself and went on about how I was checking the volunteer list for accuracy. "Will you please give me your address again?" I asked.

There was silence for a moment. Then Mr. Sibley said, "What's written down there is right."

"One forty-five Puckett Street?"

His words came out in a rush, as though he were relieved to have the address spoken. "Puckett Street. That's what it says." Had he forgotten?

"Is that the address for this telephone number?"

"That's right." Before I could ask another question Mr. Sibley said, "We're kind of busy right now. My son-in-law and his family are visiting here. He's the one who answered the phone."

"I'm sorry," I said. "I shouldn't have kept you. See you tomorrow."

He mumbled his good-byes and broke the connection.

I pulled a pen and notepad out of my desk, dialed the information number, and when the operator answered I asked, "Could you please give me the telephone number for an Edwin Sibley?" Just to make sure there'd be no mistake, I spelled it.

"Thank you," the operator said, but instead of the recorded number I expected there was silence. Finally, she said, "I'm sorry, but I have no listing for an Edwin Sibley."

"Is it an unlisted number?"

150

"I'm sorry. I am unable to give you a listing for an Edwin Sibley."

"Thank you, operator," I said, and slowly put down the receiver.

I'd been right to be suspicious of Edwin Sibley. What was he doing working in Dad's campaign office? Was he there to sabotage it?

Maybe Mr. Sibley was the one who'd spray-painted the office. He could have disposed of the paint can somewhere.

How about the other things that had happened at the office? The mailings that had disappeared? The equipment that had been misplaced? Were they accidents or sabotage? Was Mr. Sibley to blame? He was at the office every day. This could have been his work.

Mr. Sibley had gone to work as a volunteer the day after Mark's party, but I couldn't figure out how anything that had happened at the campaign office tied in with the men I'd overheard that night.

It wasn't much later when my phone rang. I was working so hard to memorize chemistry symbols that it made me jump.

Justin? was my first hope, but it was Sally Jo.

"I've found out a couple of things for you already," she said. "First of all, about Dexter Kline. I have a friend who's a secretary in the employment agency your parents used. She was only too glad to look up Dexter Kline's folder. But surprise, surprise, there wasn't one."

"But that's the agency my parents always use."

"Not this time," she said. "If you can find out the

correct one, just let me know, and I'll take it from there."

"I don't understand this," I said. "Something's not right." I remembered Edwin Sibley, so I told her what I'd discovered.

"Okay," she said. "I'll see what I can do to check him out, too."

"Thanks for calling," I told her. "You don't know how glad I am that you're helping me."

"Wait a minute," she said. "I told you I had a couple of pieces of information, and I've only given you one."

"What's the other?"

"I've got a candidate for your mystery man with the scratchy voice," she said. "I talked to our reporter who handles the Austin beat, Hank Jolie, and when I described a scratchy voice, he picked up on it right away. He described the man, and his description sounded like the one you gave me. I asked Hank if he could fax me any photos, and he said he could. He'll send them tomorrow morning."

"Who is old scratchy voice?" I asked.

"He works for Jimmy Milco. He has an ambiguous title, which doesn't mean anything." There was an edge of sarcasm in her voice as she added, "There are a number of people with ambiguous titles on the governor's personal staff."

"You didn't tell me his name," I said.

"I didn't think it would mean anything to you. You'll need to see his photos in order to know if it's the same person, and I'll bring them to your house tomorrow after school."

We were interrupted by a couple of loud clicks, and Sally Jo said, "There's my other line. I'll have to get it."

"Thanks again," I said, "but . . ."

"Oh, yeah, his name," Sally Jo said. "Nothing special. John Lamotta."

John Lamotta? His name meant no more to me than the words I'd heard him speak. Why should I be so afraid of him?

Chapter 14

Mom came upstairs and stopped by my room to kiss me good night. "Oh, honey," she murmured and held me tightly.

"I'm sorry, Mom, about scaring you and Dad," I said again.

"It's all right, Cary," Mom said. "It's over and done with and we won't talk about it." Mom looked awful, and it was my fault. I felt like a jerk.

After Mom went off to bed I read for a while, but I realized I hadn't heard Dad come upstairs, so I quietly walked down to the library and entered the open door.

Dad was sitting with his elbows propped on the desk, his forehead resting in the palms of his hands. "Dad?" I asked softly, realizing that he hadn't heard me come in.

He started, looked up at me with a bewildered expression, and said, "Isn't it past your bedtime, Cary?"

"It's eleven-thirty," I told him, but I sat in the chair across from his desk and leaned my own elbows on his desk. "I try to remember what our lives were like be-

Joan Lowery Nixon

fore you filed to run for office," I said, "and I can't. It seems like such a long time ago."

"There are bound to be changes," he began, but I interrupted.

"That's what Mom said, but it's not the changes that bother me as much as all the people who are suddenly mixed up in our lives. There are people we're afraid of, and even people who seem to have come out of nowhere."

"Out of nowhere?"

"Dexter."

"What about Dexter?"

"Dad, where did you find Dexter?"

"That's a strange question," Dad said and looked down at his hands.

This wasn't like Dad, who always was so poised, so put-together, so much in charge. Maybe it was the light in here, but his skin seemed yellowed, and his eyelids drooped with exhaustion.

"Cary," he said in a voice that was so heavy and tired it made me ache for him, "I wanted to do the right thing. I wanted to make changes which would benefit everyone in Texas. The state should be run with honor and integrity. I . . ." His voice broke, and he couldn't continue.

"What are you telling me, Dad?"

"That I have no right to cause you and your mother so much worry, to have put you into a position that might even be potentially dangerous."

"You didn't!" Dad couldn't kick out all his dreams because of me. I couldn't let him do that.

156

"I didn't foresee all the ramifications," Dad said, as though he were talking to himself. "My plan was too simplistic. I'd offer the voters my proposals for a better government, and if they accepted them and voted me into office, I'd work hard to put them into practice. Maybe I'm too used to giving orders and having them carried out. I didn't anticipate such a strong opposition and the effect it would have on my family."

I reached out and took his hands in mine. "Dad! The way you're talking, I can't tell what you have in mind. You're not giving up, are you?"

He slowly looked up at me. "I don't know, Cary," he said. "I'm trying to think it through."

"What does Mom want you to do?"

"She doesn't want me to drop out of the race."

"Then neither do I," I said. "You won't, will you?"

"I don't know yet."

"We've come this far, and Mom and I are willing to stick with it all the way."

"It won't be easy for you."

I managed to grin at him. "Hey! Being a good governor won't be easy, either."

The bare shadow of a smile touched Dad's face. He rose, took my hands, and pulled me to my feet.

I wasn't through with my pep talk. "Don't worry about that break-in, Dad. It could have happened to anyone. Don't let some creep stop you from doing what you want to do."

Even though I really didn't believe what I'd just said, I must have sounded convincing because Dad seemed to perk up, so I went on. "You're going to find that a lot

Joan Lowery Nixon

of people want you to run for governor, Dad. There'll
be big crowds at your fund-raiser Saturday, and you'll
see that I'm right."

"It's long past your bedtime, Cary," Dad told me, but
he gave me a smile, and seeing that smile made me feel
a hundred percent better. "You'll be falling asleep in
class," he said. "Hurry upstairs. Now!"

I did as he said. Dad hadn't given me the answer I'd
wanted, but I could tell that he was back on his own
track.

In the morning Dad told me he was in the race to
stay, no matter what. I was proud of him, but at the
same time I couldn't help secretly wishing he had
never got the idea of running for office.

He left for an early meeting, and Mom came in
dressed to leave, too. She was carrying a folding umbrella because it was raining. "A cold front's moving
in," she said.

"I'm not ready to leave yet," I told her and reached
for my glass of milk, ready to chugalug it.

"I'm not taking you," Mom said. "A last-minute
change of schedule. I've got to meet with my client
before he leaves to catch a plane."

"But Dad's got the other car, so Dexter can't . . ."

"I called Justin a few minutes ago and asked him to
pick you up." Mom aimed a kiss in my direction and
pulled out her car keys.

"Mom! You didn't!" She had reached the door by this
time but stopped to stare at me in surprise.

"Well, why . . . ?" She broke off. "Cary, I don't have

158

time to discuss it, although what was wrong with calling Justin I can't imagine."

I could have told her, but she was already on her way out of the house.

When Justin drove up I was waiting for him. It was a cold rain, and I pulled the collar of my red raincoat up around my neck. I hurried into his car, plopping down on the seat next to him and tossing my dripping umbrella to the floor. I didn't scoot close, the way I usually did, but kept a space between us.

"I'm sorry Mom bothered you," I told him.

"She didn't bother me," Justin said. "It's not any trouble to pick you up."

We were talking to each other as though we were strangers, and I hated it, but I didn't know how to change things.

After a couple of minutes of silence Justin turned to give me a quick glance. "Your Mom sounded kind of nervous about you, Cary, like she didn't want to let you out of her sight. How come?"

I hadn't told Justin anything about what had happened—Nora's calls, the car that followed me, the man who hid in my room—and I didn't want to. It was bad enough that we were breaking up. My private life was none of Justin's business. "It's not like that," I said and tried to change the subject. "I'm glad you got your car back. You never told me what happened after the police said they'd impound it."

"They didn't. Dad's attorney worked things out. Because we all tested clean and the call about us was anonymous, they went along with what we thought—

that someone had set us up and planted the drugs." He looked at me again. "I can't figure out who would have done it. Can you?"

"No," I answered. Believe me, I'd tried.

"I already thought of Mark," Justin said. "He's the only weirdo we know. But Mark said he didn't do it, and I think he was telling the truth. It was too rotten, even for him."

What if it had been some fanatic—someone crazy enough to try to get Dad out of the race by attacking me? I didn't know, so I didn't say any more about it, and we drove the rest of the way in silence.

I had just put my books in my locker when Mark practically yelled in my ear. "Cary! You've got to see the pictures I took at the Halloween dance!"

"No, thanks," I said. I didn't want to be reminded of that dance. Mark handed me the pictures anyway, and I handed them right back. "I'm busy, Mark. I don't want to see your pictures."

"Yes, you do," he said and shoved them in my face.

I started to shove them right back at him, but I decided the fastest way to get rid of Mark was to look at his pictures and let him go bug someone else. "Nice," I mumbled, "very nice," as I flipped through the stack. I looked awful, but I wasn't going to give Mark the satisfaction of reacting.

I was near the end of the stack when my eye caught a group of kids in the senior class. Behind them a girl with long black hair was looking directly at the camera. "Francine!" I said.

Mark hung over my shoulder. "Who? That one? Who was she? Somebody's date?"

"Somebody who shouldn't have been there," I said. I wasn't talking to Mark. I was talking to myself. The anonymous phone call to the police. The drugs planted in Justin's car. Was Francine responsible? And why? Why would she want to make me look bad and discredit Dad?

"A gate crasher?" Mark chuckled, snatched the photos out of my hand, and hurried off to give the news to someone else.

It was hard to keep my mind on what was taking place at school. The same disc jockey had started a new Charles Amberson joke: "I have all the qualities it takes to be governor—money, money, and more money." Some of the kids had picked it up, but it wasn't hard to ignore because it was childish and silly . . . and so were they for repeating it.

After the last class, I'd just pulled my coat and umbrella from my locker when Cindy Parker grabbed my arm and said, "Oh, Cary, you're just the person I need. I lost my umbrella, but there's an old one in the trunk of my car. Lend me yours so I can run out and get it. Okay?"

I held out my umbrella, but she grabbed for my coat, too. "I'd better wear this. It's really coming down hard."

Typically Cindy. I wasn't surprised.

Allie had come up behind Cindy, and she and I walked to the door. A few of the kids had sprinted to their cars, but some of them waited, as we did, hoping the downpour would let up in a few minutes.

As I watched Cindy run across the lot, the umbrella pulled so close that she looked like a red mushroom with feet, I noticed a sedan pull from the far end of the lot. It began to pick up speed, and as I stared, unable to believe what I was seeing, the driver aimed right for Cindy.

I dropped my books and ran through the door, screaming at the top of my lungs, "Cindy! Look out!"

Chapter 15

She couldn't have heard me, but maybe she heard the car, because she looked up and saw it. Only a second later she flew over the hood of the car parked next to her. I couldn't tell if the driver had hit Cindy or if she'd been able to fling herself out of the way.

I should have tried to get the license number, but the car sped out of the lot faster than I could think. I yelled for help and ran toward Cindy.

Some of the other kids came running, too, and we knelt around Cindy, whose chin and nose were skinned and oozing blood. She lay on the asphalt crying. "My leg," she said. "Don't touch me! I think my leg's broken."

I pulled out a Kleenex to hold to her face, but it was rain-soaked in an instant. Someone had run to the office, and Coach Mac was the first faculty member to arrive. "An ambulance is coming, Cindy," he said, and he turned to the rest of us. "You kids, clear out of the way. Go on back inside. Move it!"

At first I was too paralyzed to obey him, but someone

163

took a firm grip on my arm and pulled me around, walking me across the parking lot.

I looked up through a blur of tears and rain to see Justin. "It's my fault. She had on my coat. They thought she was me," I babbled.

Justin didn't say anything until he'd opened the door of his car and shoved me inside. "Stay here, and I'll get your books," he said.

In just a couple of minutes he was back. He threw my books in the back seat and reached for an old sweatshirt, which he handed to me. "You can mop up with this," he said.

I tried, wiping my face, but my hair dripped down my shoulders and back, and I shivered. I couldn't stop shaking.

"Here," Justin said, and he wrapped his jacket around me. For the first time I saw that he was as wet as I was, and I leaned against his shoulder, his arms snugly around me, and cried.

We heard a siren, and in just a couple of minutes a police car arrived. Right on its heels was an ambulance.

I sat up. "I'd better talk to the police."

"Did you get the license number?"

"No. I need to tell them that the driver thought Cindy was me."

"You're not going to tell them some fool thing like that, Cary," Justin said. He pulled away, turned on the ignition, and drove slowly out of the school's parking lot.

"It's *not* a fool thing!" I said. "Justin, someone's after me. They tried to scare me. They broke into my bedroom. And now this. If Cindy hadn't jumped out of the way, she would have been killed!"

We came to a boulevard stop, and as he turned to look at me I could see that Justin was scared. "You really think so?"

"Why else would that driver have just aimed for Cindy? It wasn't an accident."

"It may have been some nut who didn't care who he hit, or someone after Cindy."

"No, Justin," I said. "The driver thought Cindy was me."

"I don't get it."

"Please. Just trust me. I'll go into it later." I put a hand on Justin's arm. "I need to talk to Cindy. Will you take me to see her?"

"We'll have to find out which hospital she'll be in. We'd better get into dry clothes first."

"Thanks," I said.

I leaned back against the seat and closed my eyes, but Justin said, "Cary, don't get me wrong. Sometimes I don't put things the right way. What I mean is, I'm sorry that Cindy got hurt, but I'm glad it wasn't you. I don't know what I'd do if anything happened to you."

He reached over and took my hand, and I held it tightly all the way home.

I found Velma in the kitchen.

"Well, look at you," she said. She did a double take and demanded, "Wait a minute! How'd you get in a state like that? What did you do with your coat and umbrella?"

"I lent them to a friend."

Joan Lowery Nixon

Velma shook her head as if I were a dork beyond help. "Better get into a hot shower right away. And take some vitamin C."

As I left the kitchen she called after me, "That lady reporter came by just a few minutes ago. She left an envelope for you. It's on the front-hall table. She said she had to go out of town for an interview and she might not get to see you until tomorrow."

I picked up the envelope and carried it upstairs. Just the tip of the gummed flap was sealed, and I was tempted to open it.

First things first. I had to hurry because Justin would be coming. I tossed the envelope on the bed, but I had second thoughts. I didn't know why, and I felt a little stupid about what I was doing, but I put the envelope under the stacks of T-shirts and shorts in the bottom drawer of my chest of drawers, making sure it was well hidden.

The steaming water took away the chill, but I was still shivering from fear. What would I say to Cindy? Should I tell her she'd been mistaken for me? No. That would sound dumb. There'd be too many things to explain, too many questions without answers.

I needed Cindy to tell me what she saw. I hoped she could describe the driver of that car. Had anyone got the license number? If they had, Cindy's family would probably know.

Carrying a warm coat and another umbrella, I waited in the entry hall for Justin. From the corner of my eye I caught a movement and whirled to face Dexter the Silent.

166

"Are you going with your parents to the party tonight in Fort Worth?" he asked.

"Yes, I am," I answered. Mom had mentioned it—Fort Worth's chance to meet the party's three candidates. We'd have barbecue and a Western band, and she thought I'd have fun. But with all that had happened, that particular celebration had gone out of my mind. I didn't feel like a party. I hoped Mom and Dad wouldn't care if I didn't go.

"I assume you'll also be attending the fund-raiser for your father on Friday?"

I assume you'll be attending! Sometimes I got the feeling that Dexter tried too hard to sound like a butler-chauffeur. I kept a straight face and answered firmly, "Yes. I'll be there. That's the big night, and Dad's going to give an important speech."

I knew the speech would include whatever Dad's investigators had discovered about the awarding of construction contracts and payoffs to Jimmy Milco, but I didn't know what all of that information was. I suppose I could have told Dexter that much, but because I was suspicious of him, I didn't want to tell him anything.

However, there was something I could *ask* him! Hoping to catch him off guard, I blurted out, "Dexter, where are you really from?"

Instead of a simple, direct answer, he queried me in turn, "Exactly what do you mean?"

I couldn't tell him that Sally Jo and I had done some checking up on him and found that the employment agency didn't have his name in their files. I was stuck, so

I mumbled, "You know. Like, have you always lived in Dallas?"

"Dallas is my home," he said.

That didn't tell me anything. Did he mean it's my home *now,* or I was born here, or I've lived here ten years?

Okay. Have it your way, I thought. But I'm not through with you.

I didn't talk much after Justin and I entered the hospital. Hospitals have a way of making you feel you should whisper and tiptoe. Fortunately, Cindy's door was open because I wouldn't have known whether to knock or just wait quietly until someone opened it. Cindy was propped up on pillows, one ankle in a cast, and her mother was seated by the bed, holding her hand.

There were already bouquets of flowers in the room and a big box of chocolates, and I was embarrassed. We should have brought something.

We said hello to Mrs. Parker, but I hung back, afraid to touch Cindy in case I hurt her even more. "I'm terribly sorry!" I said.

Cindy's smile was a little lopsided, probably because of pain pills. "It doesn't hurt now," she said. "The doctor told me what was broken, but I can't remember what he called it. Anyhow, it was just a hairline fracture." Her smile suddenly drooped. "I'm afraid I ruined your coat, Cary."

"Don't even think about my coat! The coat's not important! That driver could have killed you!"

Mrs. Parker leaned forward. "Did you see him, Cary?"

"No," I said.

She persisted. "Did you get the license?"

"I didn't try to get the license. I'm sorry. I was looking at Cindy. I was trying to get to her before . . ."

"I understand." Mrs. Parker's shoulders sagged. "No one saw a license plate, and no one can identify the driver. I can't imagine what that man was doing on your school grounds."

I turned to Cindy. "You saw him?"

She shook her head. "Not really. Just enough to know it was a man who was driving and not a woman."

"Did he have dark hair? Light hair?"

"I have no idea. I saw the car coming straight toward me, and I got the impression that a man was driving. That's it. And then I jumped."

She jumped! Great! I felt a lot better knowing that the car hadn't touched her.

Justin and I talked with Cindy and her mother another five minutes, then some of her relatives came by, so we said good-bye and left. We stopped off in the gift shop, picked out a huge teddy bear and a bottle of cologne, and arranged to have our gifts sent to Cindy's room. Thank goodness for credit cards!

As we walked to Justin's car I said, "I hoped Cindy could tell me something about the driver."

"You've only told me part of the story," Justin said. "You said I should trust you and you'd fill me in on the rest of it later."

During the drive home I did just that.

"I don't get *why* someone is doing this," Justin said.

"It all started the day after Mark's party," I told him. "I'm guessing it must be because of something they think I overheard on the terrace."

"You said what you heard wasn't important. You told me that the night of Mark's party."

"I hadn't thought about what it meant," I said.

"Can you do that now?"

I went over the whole conversation. "That's what I heard. That's it. Does any of it mean anything to you?"

Justin thought a moment, then shook his head. "No," he said. He pulled up in front of our house, and I climbed out of the car. The rain had let up, and the grass and shrubbery glistened. I took a deep breath of the cool, clean air.

"Don't you want me to come in?" he asked. "Cary, I won't leave you alone for a minute, if you think it will help."

I ducked back into the car and gave him the kind of kiss I'd been missing so much. "There'll be plenty of people around," I said, "but I promise I'll call on you any time I need you." I sat back and grinned. "And then some."

He gave me a lingering kiss good-bye, and I reluctantly pulled out my front-door key. But the door opened before I could use it.

"Hi," Mom said. "I saw Justin driving off." She gave me a hug and asked, "Now. Tell me. Why wasn't I supposed to ask Justin to give you a ride this morning?"

I just smiled and said, "No reason. You can ask him to give me a lift any time."

170

Mom looked a little puzzled, but she didn't push. Instead, she said, "It took you long enough to get home from school."

"We came home to change clothes. Then we went to the hospital to see Cindy Parker. She broke her leg."

"Oh, good gracious!" Mom said. "I'll have to call Mrs. Parker. How is Cindy feeling?"

"She's feeling pretty good. She said it was only a hairline fracture."

I expected Mom to ask how it happened, but she said, "You can tell me all the details later. I'm really running late. I've got to get ready for that Fort Worth barbecue."

I was glad to escape an explanation. They were excited about the party. This was a big night for both of them. I couldn't ruin it by telling them that I suspected the driver was not after Cindy but was after me.

Dad arrived home a few minutes later. He greeted me and asked, "Where is Laura?"

"Upstairs, getting ready for Fort Worth." I tagged up the stairs behind him and, when we reached the top, said, "Do I have to go?"

"I thought you'd want to."

"Not really." I told him that Cindy had been hurt and had a broken leg. I added, "It's like I've been holding my breath all day, and now that I've let it out, I'm tired."

He smiled. "Stay home if you wish. The barbecue will be good, but the speeches won't be that exciting."

"Are you going to say anything about Governor Milco?"

"I've got some good solid information about him," Dad said. "I'm afraid it goes beyond Milco and his friends just lining their pockets with taxpayer money through construction kickbacks and blatant favoritism. But I'll make that proof public in the speech I'll give at the fund-raiser banquet on Friday, because there will be good television and newspaper coverage. Tonight I'll speak about education reforms."

"What about Ben Cragmore's construction company?"

"We're working on that, but it has to be done the hard way. We still haven't found the missing superintendent who can be our chief witness and who'll tie it all together for us."

"When you do tell everyone about what Milco and his friends are doing, will they arrest Governor Milco?"

"No."

"Why not?"

"First, the state's attorney general would have to bring charges. Since he's in the governor's party and was elected on Milco's coattails, he's likely to delay on taking any action."

That made me mad! "Well, at least the voters won't vote for Milco when they find out what he's done!"

Dad gave me a rueful smile. "I'm afraid you need a more realistic view of history, Cary. Some voters will vote for anyone who's in the 'right' party, and many voters will vote for a name that sounds familiar, not knowing anything about the person for whom they're voting."

I shuddered. "Politics, yuck!"

"I've heard that before," Dad said with a smile.

I grinned back. But then I wondered, what was so funny? Not politics!

I ran back downstairs to see what there was to eat. I didn't want Velma to have to go to the trouble of making a special dinner just for me. She probably had planned a meal just for Dexter and herself. I didn't feel like a big meal anyway, so I decided to stay out of the way and let her think I'd been taken care of.

Velma wasn't in the kitchen, so I made myself a peanut butter and strawberry jam sandwich, dumped some potato chips on the plate, and added an apple. There was just about enough butter pecan ice cream for one big serving in the carton, so I tucked it in one arm, managed to hang onto a can of diet soda, and headed for my bedroom. There was a well-balanced meal. Did I know my basic food groups, or what!

I was busy doing my English lit homework and polishing off the ice cream when Mom and Dad came in to say good night.

"I'll get out the car," Dad said and left.

But Mom hesitated. "Have you got enough light?" she asked. "That desk lamp reaches such a small area."

"It's enough, Mom," I said. "The desk is the only place where I'm working."

"I can turn on the overhead light."

"Then it's too glary. I'm fine, Mom. Honest."

Mom bent and kissed my forehead. "See you later, honey," she said, and gently shut my bedroom door when she left.

It was quiet in the house. The telephone wasn't ringing because I'd taken it off the hook. I would have liked to talk to Allie, but I absolutely had to catch up on my homework. I knew that Velma would be snug in her apartment off the kitchen, watching her usual television programs. Dexter, of course, would have gone to his garage apartment right after an early dinner. It was wonderful, for a change, to have a quiet house that wasn't filled with people. And I didn't have to worry. The police were keeping an eye on the house. Occasionally I'd seen a police car drive past, and I was awfully glad to know they were nearby.

An hour later there was nothing left to eat, and I was practically falling asleep over some long poem by Robert Browning, which at the moment wasn't making sense, when I heard the small squeak of the creaking board outside my door.

As I reached up and snapped off my lamp, the darkness swooped in, smothering me. My throat was dry, and I was afraid to breathe. I sat very still while my eyes grew used to the dark. I waited. And waited. And listened intently for another sound.

A narrow streak of light from the hallway lay like a bright border at the bottom of my door, but as I watched, a shadow broke it, then another.

Someone was standing right outside my bedroom door!

Chapter 16

Frantically, I looked toward the telephone, but it would take too long to hang up, wait for a dial tone, and call 911. And it would make too much noise. Whoever was in this house was waiting and listening, too.

At any minute he was going to enter my bedroom, and there was nowhere I could hide.

But as I stared at the shadow, holding my breath as he shifted his feet, it came to me that there was one place in which he wouldn't see me if he opened the door. I'd hide *behind* the door.

Carefully and slowly, I stepped closer and closer to the door and the shadow, knowing that at any moment the person outside the door might open it, and we'd be face to face. Numb with terror, I saw the doorknob begin to turn, and I slid into place against the wall just as the door opened. My heart pounded. *Please,* I begged, *don't let him hear it!*

The shadow, accented by the light in the hall, stretched its long dark limbs across my carpet and grew into the figure of a man who walked into the middle of

Joan Lowery Nixon

my room. Cautiously, he turned his head from left to right as he scanned the room, and I could easily see who he was. Dexter.

What did he think he was doing, creeping into my room!

I couldn't confront him here. I didn't know what he had in mind. I only knew that I needed help. And soon. At any moment he might turn around and discover my hiding place.

I moved forward stealthily, squeezing around the edge of the door. Then I ran, my adrenaline pumping like super-fuel, propelling me down the stairs.

"Cary!" Dexter shouted. "Stop!" He was right behind me.

I jumped the last three steps and ran across the entry hall, yelling, "Help! Velma! Help me!"

But a hand came down on my shoulder, and I was spun around so hard I fell against Dexter.

He righted me, keeping his grip on my shoulder, as he said, "I didn't mean to scare you. I didn't know you were home. I thought you'd gone with your parents."

I could hardly get the words out. "What are you going to do?"

"Apologize," he said. "That's what I'm trying to do."

"Why were you in my room?" I took a deep breath and tried to speak more normally.

"I thought I heard someone upstairs. I had to check it out, so I went upstairs to look around."

"I wasn't making any noise. I was just sitting there, reading." I jerked my shoulder, trying to pull away, and Dexter released his grip.

176

A Candidate for Murder

"You may not have been aware of making noise," he said. He stood a little straighter, held his chin a little higher, and assumed his usual expression of detachment. "One's chair squeaks; one brushes a foot against the desk. It's easy not to notice."

Dexter was back to being a butler, but I knew he wasn't a real one. I'd caught him off guard, and now I was sure. He was a fake.

What was he *really* doing upstairs while he thought Mom and Dad and I were out of the house?

Velma scurried into the entry hall, fumbling with the tie on her robe. "What's the matter, Cary?" she asked. "What are you doing here? I thought you were in Fort Worth with your parents."

"I'm afraid I unwittingly startled Miss Caroline," Dexter told Velma. "I believed that the entire family had gone, so when I heard a car pull into the drive, then leave, I wanted to be positive that the house was secure. I was in the living room when I heard a sound over my head, so I went upstairs to find out what it was and, in the process, I frightened Miss Caroline."

I wished he'd stop talking like that. He didn't have to. I'd heard him when he'd dropped the butler pose.

I realized that Velma was looking at me, waiting for whatever I'd have to say. What could I do except go along with Dexter's smooth explanation? "It was about like that," I mumbled. "I didn't know Dexter was in the house."

"Why didn't you go to the barbecue?" Velma's thoughts made an abrupt shift. "Oh, my, you didn't have dinner. Are you hungry? Do you want something to eat?"

"No, thanks," I said. I looked at Velma, unwilling to meet Dexter's eyes, and mumbled, "I'm sorry I got so upset and made so much noise. Okay?"

"Okay," Velma said and smiled reassuringly.

"Of course," Dexter said. His steady gaze felt like lasers boring into my skull.

Velma. The envelope. I suddenly remembered. Velma had told me that Sally Jo brought it, and I'd taken it upstairs and hidden it. Was that envelope what Dexter had been after? Or was it me?

"Good night," I said and made a dash for the stairs. Once I was safely inside my room, I carefully locked the door.

I slipped the envelope from under the clothes in the bottom drawer and dumped out the contents on my desk, under the reading lamp. There was a short note from Sally Jo in which she said she was enclosing a computer printout about Ben Cragmore.

"I skimmed some of it," she wrote, "but didn't have time to go through it in detail. We can do this tomorrow. John Lamotta is in each of the pictures. Do you recognize him?"

Did I ever!

There were three newspaper photographs—small groups of men—and even though the faxed copies weren't as clear as real photographs, there was no mistaking the man I'd seen with Ben Cragmore.

And there was no mistaking the girl in the fourth

photograph. The caption underneath that photo identified her as Francine Lamotta, John Lamotta's daughter.

I read through the printout next. There were a million uninteresting things in it about Ben Cragmore. I did find out that he'd been before a grand jury a couple of times but hadn't been indicted. There was something about a sale of stock under question and about falsified receipts on supplies, but he'd never been officially charged, and he'd never gone to trial. However, he'd been sued at least a half-dozen times by other firms. Twice he'd lost and had to pay up. One case was still on appeal.

He'd had companies and partnerships under a number of names, and all his partners and company officers were listed. I studied the lists of names carefully. Lamotta was there, but it wasn't John. It was Francine. I bet her father hid behind her name. It was easy to see why Mr. Lamotta couldn't let it be known he was one of Ben Cragmore's partners, since he was on the governor's staff and probably had a lot of influence in deciding where contracts would be awarded.

There was information about Mr. Cragmore's professional and social clubs; the taxes he paid; the value of his property; and even the members of his family, which included a wife, Mabel Broussard Cragmore, three grown children, Ben, Jr., Robert, and William, a brother, Horace, and Mabel's mother, Nora Broussard.

Nora!

I nearly swept the papers off the desk. Nora! It had to be the Nora who'd called me, didn't it? The Nora who'd know why I was in danger. The printout even listed all their addresses.

I had to talk to Nora. She held the key to this whole thing. Nora had wanted to talk to me before but had chickened out. I might get her to change her mind and tell me what she'd wanted to say. Should I tell that detective, Jim Slater, about Nora? No. I was sure Nora would never talk to the police.

I called Justin. "You said you'd help me," I told him.

"I will," he said. "Anything you want, Cary."

"I think I found out who Nora is. I want to go and see her."

"Right now?"

"No," I said. "Can you make it after school tomorrow?"

"Sure. Want me to pick you up, too?"

"Yes," I said. "I'd like that a lot." I wished I could reach through the phone and hug him. Everything was better than ever between Justin and me. He couldn't possibly know how lonely I'd been without him. I was selfish enough to hope that he'd missed me just as much.

All everybody at school could talk about was Cindy and the crazy driver. It hadn't occurred to anyone that the driver's actions were deliberate. Things like that didn't happen at schools like ours.

After classes, when I climbed into Justin's car, I said, "Could we stop by the campaign office for just a couple of minutes, first? I've got some questions to ask Mr. Sibley."

Justin grimaced. "As long as those women don't make me carry heavy boxes around."

"You can stay in the car if you want to. I won't be long."

Justin parked on Commerce Street, just a few doors from the office, and I went inside. As I came through the front doors, I saw Mr. Sibley going down the hallway toward the back offices.

I followed him, but Delia grabbed my arm and managed to pat my shoulder at the same time. "Thank goodness you're here," she said, as she steered me toward a table near the back of the room. "There are jillions of things to get done, and two of our steady helpers are home with some kind of virus."

"I can't stay," I told her. "I just stopped by for something."

Delia rolled her eyes as though it was all she could expect from me and strode toward the front door to greet a woman who had just come in. I ducked down the hallway after Mr. Sibley.

He saw me, I know he did, but he scooped up a large, heavy cardboard box that was probably filled with trash and staggered with it out the back door into the alley. Good. A private place where we could talk was exactly what I wanted.

I slipped through the door just before it shut. "Mr. Sibley, could I please talk to you?" I asked.

His eyes were frightened. He dropped the box on the ground, looked to each side as though searching for an escape route, then suddenly slumped, his shoulders rounding, as though he'd given up.

Joan Lowery Nixon

"What's the matter, Mr. Sibley?" I asked him. "I just want to talk."

"You want to ask me questions about the address I gave." He sounded so defeated I hurt for him.

I spoke softly, the way I would to a skittish animal. "Yes. I wondered why you gave the address of a vacant store on a nonresidential street."

"Because I'm no longer clever," he said. "I picked a street name at random from the Dallas phone book. I should have chosen the right kind of house on the right kind of street. Then no one would have suspected."

"I don't understand," I told him. "You gave a phone number where you could be reached but the wrong address."

He raised his head and looked into my eyes. "And you want to know why. Is it so important?"

"I wouldn't ask if it wasn't."

He just stared at me for a few moments, his pupils distorted and blurry behind the thick lenses, so I said, "Mr. Sibley, there have been some—some threats." I didn't know what to call them.

At this he jerked as though he'd been given an electric shock. His voice was a whisper as he asked, "You think I've had something to do with threats?"

Mr. Sibley sat on an upturned crate near the trash bin and rested his forearms on his thighs. "These clothes I wear," he said. "Have you ever wondered why I wear the same clothes, day after day?"

Of course I had, but I couldn't tell him that, so I didn't answer.

"I wash my shirt and iron it each day. I take my pants

182

and vest to the dry cleaner when I can because I have no other clothes suitable to wear to this office, only a set of khaki work clothes to change into."

"Mr. Sibley," I began, miserable at his embarrassment, but he interrupted me.

"The telephone is not in my name because I don't live in a home of my own. I live in a recovery house, a halfway shelter for former drug abusers."

"Oh," I mumbled and frantically searched for the right thing to say. I couldn't find it.

He sat upright, and again his eyes met mine. "I used to be a successful accountant for an oil company—not your father's," he quickly added. "But I'll never be able to go back to the kind of life where I work and socialize with intelligent and interesting people. This political volunteer work is the closest I can come to the lifestyle I once knew."

Tears came to his eyes, and he grunted, "Now this is over, too."

"No!" I cried out. "I won't tell anyone what you told me. I promise!"

"I believe in your father's ideas," he said as his face flushed a deep red, "even his tough stance against drugs."

"Then please keep working for him," I begged.

Mr. Sibley got to his feet and tried to lift the large cardboard box up over his head to drop it into the trash bin, but it was so heavy he couldn't raise it that high. I hurried to help him, taking one side of the box, but just in time I jerked it back, nearly knocking poor Mr. Sibley off his feet as I shouted, "Stop! Wait! These are some of the brochures!"

Mr. Sibley stared at the contents of the box in astonishment and blushed again. "It was next to the trash box," he said. "I picked up the wrong box. I made a mistake."

I hoisted the box into my arms and walked to the back door, waiting while Mr. Sibley opened it for me.

"I make mistakes sometimes, even though I try not to," he whispered, and I hurt, not knowing how to answer him.

We couldn't just put the box back quietly. Coming through the door, we bumped head-on into Delia.

"What's this?" she asked and took possession of the box.

"I picked up the wrong box," Mr. Sibley said. "I won't do it again."

"Thank you." Delia spoke with an exaggerated distinctness. As Mr. Sibley scurried out the door, this time with the box of trash, she muttered, "Oh, what I have to go through!" and looked to the heavens. Then, in almost the same tone of voice, she said to me, "Are you coming here to work tomorrow?"

"I'll try to." I moved close to Delia and quietly asked, "What do you know about Mr. Sibley?"

"Not much," she said. "As I remember, Edwin's son-in-law told me there were some health problems, but he reassured me that Edwin would be a good, conscientious worker."

"His son-in-law?"

"Yes," Delia snapped with impatience. "Edwin lives with his daughter and son-in-law."

I was too stunned to speak. I tried to go over what Mr. Sibley had told me. What kind of story had he given me? And if it was right, then what kind of garbage had that supposed son-in-law told Delia?

I didn't have the answer.

So far I'd been getting nothing but phony stories from those I'd questioned: Dexter and Mr. Sibley. Would I do any better when I talked to Nora?

Nora Broussard lived in a block of apartments. Behind a bus stop the entrance to the main building was impressive with huge colonial pillars and brass lamps, but tiny apartment windows skittered out to either side like poor relations. Justin and I parked under the overhang and followed the arrows to the door with the large brass plate inscribed OFFICE.

We walked through a narrow foyer, its inner wall filled with rows and rows of mailboxes, and entered a large lobby. The lobby was decorated in whites and blues and lots of chrome, and a woman who looked as though she tried to follow the same color scheme, from her huge balloon of white hair to her blue dress, watched us as we crossed the thick carpet to her desk.

"Could you please give us Mrs. Nora Broussard's apartment number?" I asked her.

She shook her head. "We respect our residents' privacy," she said.

"It's important that I talk to her."

"I'm very sorry I can't help you," she said, but she didn't sound the least bit sorry. She sounded smug, as though she'd been waiting all week for a chance to turn someone down.

Justin gave a tug to my elbow, but I ignored it. "Please," I begged the woman. "I *have* to see her."

"Sorry," she said. She pulled something out of her desk and began to write. It was probably a poison-pen letter.

This time Justin not only tugged harder, he said, "Cary, let's go," in a voice that meant business.

As we walked out of the lobby and into the foyer he pointed to the mailboxes and whispered, "Look. There's your answer."

Of course! Each mailbox had a name and number on it. We quickly scanned the names until we came to *Broussard.* Number 426.

We followed garden pathways that wound through the buildings in this large apartment complex. The four-hundred building was at the very back, an alley running behind it.

Justin and I climbed a stairway with concrete steps and wrought-iron railings that were beginning to rust. On the second floor the first apartment was 420, the next 422. Mrs. Broussard's apartment should be the fourth.

I knocked at the door and waited, but there was only silence. A very tiny, very old woman peered out of a crack in the door marked 424. "I'm looking for Mrs. Nora Broussard," I said, but she shook her head.

"I'm not Mrs. Broussard. I'm Althea Krump."

"I know," I started to say, but she interrupted.

"How could you know who I am? I've never met you before in my life."

"I meant I know that you're not Mrs. Broussard."

"It won't do any good, your knocking on her door, because she's not home."

"Do you know when she'll be back?"

"Of course not." Her face crumpled into tight wrinkles that might have meant a frown or a grin. "And don't yell," she said. "Just because I'm old doesn't mean I'm deaf!"

"I'm sorry," I told her.

I guess my apology satisfied her because she nodded to herself for a moment, then said to me, "Nora could be over to her daughter's. Mabel's married to that contractor, you know. Lots of money there, but he's tight with a dollar. He could do a lot better by his mother-in-law, but don't count on it." She paused. "Maybe he thinks she'll drink it away. Well, she probably would—most of it."

I had found the right Nora. My heart gave a jump of excitement.

"Do you know when Mrs. Broussard is usually home?"

Mrs. Krump shook her head. "I don't keep tabs on my neighbors," she said. "I keep to myself. I'm not a bother to anybody."

"Do you have Mrs. Broussard's phone number?"

"No," she said. "Not that I don't try to be friendly, but some people can be mighty stuck up. Why, the way she prisses around here you'd think she had something to be conceited about."

I pulled a scrap of paper and a pen out of my shoulder bag and wrote down my name and telephone number. "Mrs. Krump, it's very important that I reach Mrs. Broussard. Please, will you give her this? Will you ask her to call me?"

As we left I didn't hear Mrs. Krump's door close, and I knew she was watching us.

"Do you think she'll give Mrs. Broussard your phone number?" Justin asked as soon as we were out of earshot.

"She probably will," I answered, "because it will make her feel important and because then Mrs. Broussard will have to speak to her."

"I guess it's worth a try," Justin said. "The only alternative is to stick around here until Mrs. Broussard gets back, and that could take hours."

We had reached the drive in front of the apartment house, and I climbed into Justin's car. As he drove around the pillars and headed toward home I asked, "Want to come to dinner?"

"Can't," he said. "I've got a science club meeting tonight. What about tomorrow night?"

"Tomorrow's the big fund-raiser." I moved a little closer and tilted my head to look up at him. "Come with me. There'll be some boring speeches, but most of it will be fun. There's going to be a band, and dancing, and some great food."

Justin looked as though he planned to turn me down, but he suddenly laughed. "Why not?" he said.

"You won't mind the speeches?"

"I probably will," he admitted, "but I've got this feel-

188

ing, Cary, more than I ever had, that I just want to be with you. I guess I can live through a speech or two."

"Oh, Justin," I said. For a couple of seconds I got choked up. I wanted Dad to win. I wanted him to be governor of Texas. But if he did win, I'd be moving away from Justin. I didn't think I could stand that.

When I arrived home dinner wasn't ready. Velma was lifting lids on the pots and fussing at whatever was cooking inside. Was everyone in a bad mood today?

"Dexter *would* have to go across town at a busy time like this," she muttered at what smelled like carrots and slammed down the lid before they could answer back.

"Let me help you," I said. "Want me to set the table?"

"It's set, and I don't need nothin' right now. Maybe in about ten minutes or so you could lend me a hand in gettin' the food on the table."

"Sure," I told her. "I'll be glad to."

Velma smiled, her frustrations vanishing. "All right," she said. "Stick close and I'll give you a holler when I'm ready."

"When will Dexter be back?"

"Probably not for another half hour."

I turned to leave the kitchen, but Velma called after me, "That lady reporter telephoned and left a message for you. She won't get back to Dallas until tomorrow. She'll get in touch with you when she does."

There was so much I needed to tell Sally Jo. Why did she have to go out of town right now?

Well, I wasn't going to just sit and wait until she came back. I had other plans. I checked my watch and tried to walk casually without hurrying. I'd have time to take a look in Dexter's apartment, to see if I could find out more about him, and I didn't want anyone to even guess at what I had in mind.

I knew where the extra house keys were kept, on a hidden nail in a cabinet in the storeroom. I found the key for the lock on Dexter's door, grabbed it, and ran across the driveway. I climbed the outside stairs to the entrance to his apartment, fitted the key into the lock, and threw the door open.

Fortunately, the window shades were up, so there was enough light streaming into the room from the outside lamps to help me distinguish shapes from shadows. I closed the door and leaned against it, for the first time letting my glance sweep across Dexter's living room.

By squinting I could make out the sofa and chair grouping against the right-hand wall. There was nothing on the coffee table, no magazines, no books, no personal things. Built-in shelves on the wall facing me were completely empty.

Feeling as if I were viewing a room in which no one lived, I let my gaze drift to a large rocking chair at the left side of the room.

There in the chair sat Dexter, the narrow slits of his eyes glinting in the darkness like a cat's as he stared at me.

Chapter 17

I gasped, tried to speak, but lost my voice and had to start again. "I-I know I shouldn't be here," I stammered.

I expected Dexter to say something or do something while I tried to think up a good excuse for breaking into his apartment, but he didn't move.

That scared me even more. What if he was dead? I whirled and fumbled for the light switch, then shielded my eyes against the immediate brightness.

Dexter suddenly stirred, a puzzled look on his face as though he'd been awakened from sleep. "Cary?" he asked, and as he struggled to his feet the small pillow that had been behind his head fell to the floor.

"Miss Caroline," he said formally, taking a step toward me, "is something wrong?"

My hand was on the doorknob. "Uh—Velma wondered if you were home. She's almost ready to serve dinner."

I didn't wait to hear what he'd say. I threw the door open and clattered down the stairs, not stopping until I was back in the storeroom, with Dexter's key carefully tucked into place.

Would Dexter tell Mom or Dad what I'd done? I didn't think so. I suspected that Dexter had more to lose than I had. There was something strange about a man who had no personal possessions, who pretended to be a butler when he wasn't, and who slept with his eyes open.

At dinner, while Dexter served as correctly as always, the two of us avoided each other's eyes. What was he thinking about my breaking into his apartment? I really didn't want to know.

Dad told Mom he'd had a call from Governor Jimmy Milco.

"I've given the press a general idea of what I'm going to say in my speech tomorrow," Dad said. "Of course, it got back to Milco, and he's upset about the charges I plan to make."

"What did he say?" Mom asked.

"That whatever claims I made would be construed as slander. He blustered a little and threatened legal action."

"But you have proof."

"As much as I can get with so many people trying to cover things up."

"What if he sues you?"

"He has the right." Dad's voice was solemn as he added, "I don't like to hurt anyone, Laura, but the taxpayers should know that their governor is concerned with benefiting himself and not them."

"It bothers me that he'd threaten you," Mom said.

A Candidate for Murder

"Don't worry about Jimmy Milco," Dad told her. He squeezed Mom's hand and smiled. "The voters are going to put him and his cohorts out of business."

I hoped Dad was right. After dinner, before he had to leave for *another* meeting, I made sure that Dexter wasn't around and took Dad aside.

"What do you know about Dexter?" I asked Dad.

He looked surprised. The door to the library was shut, but I lowered my voice anyway. "I don't think he's really a butler."

Dad studied me before he asked, "Why not?"

"That formal way of his—he fakes it. I can tell."

"You mean if he tries hard to behave the way a butler should behave, then that means he isn't a butler?"

I scrunched up my face and groaned. "Dad, that isn't what I meant."

"It's what you said."

"Okay, okay." I gave a dramatic sigh. "Why does it sound so different when you say it and when I say it?"

Dad picked up his briefcase, slipped some papers into it, and kissed the top of my head. "Don't look for problems, Cary. There are enough real ones that need solving."

Problems? This whole campaign was a problem. It was the questions without answers that frightened me.

When I went to bed I made sure my windows were locked and, probably for the first time ever, locked my bedroom door. Even then, it was hard to sleep. I jumped at every little sound the house made as it settled in the cooler night air.

I thought of Mr. Sibley with a sense of sorrow as I

resolved the questions I'd had about him. He had lied—no doubt about it—but to Delia, not to me. Poor Mr. Sibley had been trying so hard to hide the truth of where he lived, he'd invented a son-in-law, and, obviously, someone who'd wanted to help him had played the part.

My mind skipped from one thing to another, as I lay awake waiting for my telephone to ring. Nora Broussard *had* to call me. She'd want to, wouldn't she? What had she wanted to tell me? I fell asleep asking myself that question.

When the phone jangled me awake, I groped for it and squinted at the clock. Two fifty-five. Rubbing my eyes with one hand, I managed to mumble something into the phone.

The voice was slurred again, but I knew who it was. "Why did you come nosing around here?" she asked. "Are you that stupid?"

I was awake in a hurry and sat up in bed, cupping the phone and keeping my voice down. With two closed doors and a hall between us I didn't think that Mom and Dad could hear me, but I didn't want to take chances.

"You called me," I told her. "You wanted to tell me something." She didn't answer, so I said, "I think you wanted to warn me."

"That's what I'm doing now! Don't come around here anymore!"

"I need to know what you were going to tell me."

"You know too much already. And they know you know." She made a strange kind of burble, a cross between a hiccup and a sob.

"Are you all right?"

Mrs. Broussard let out a long sigh and mumbled, "They aren't nice people. I told my daughter, 'you're letting yourself in for a lot of trouble,' I said. He hits her sometimes, you know. She shouldn't have to put up with that. Maybe Herb Gillian wouldn't have been so quick to want to blow the whistle if it hadn't been for him being there when Ben hit her."

She rambled on for a while. Mostly it was about her daughter and son-in-law, but I tried to keep track of two things she'd talked about.

Finally I broke in. "Mrs. Broussard, you said these people you're talking about think I know something. Know what?"

There was silence for a moment. Suddenly her voice switched to a nasal whine. "I told them, she wouldn't know. So she caught a word or two by accident. She couldn't put them together, I said. Leave her be. She's just a kid. It's a terrible thing to want to take away those years she's got ahead of her."

Chills snaked up my back. "You mean they want to kill me?"

She began to cry. "It's too late. They don't listen to me. No one ever did." She blew her nose loudly and said, "I've got to go."

"Wait! Not yet!" I clung to the name she had spoken. "Tell me, please, what do you know about Herb Gillian?"

"Ohhh," she moaned, and I could almost see her rocking herself back and forth, crying into the telephone. "He shouldn't have said anything. Poor Gil. Poor Gil."

She hung up, but I sat without moving, my jaw hanging open. The words came back to me. "I never thought Gil would—" "Well, now he won't."

No wonder Ben Cragmore and John Lamotta wanted to get rid of me! I'd overheard them talking about a murder!

Chapter 18

I let Mom and Dad sleep, although I dozed sitting up, my ears cocked for sounds that didn't belong, and there were plenty of them. I didn't realize how much noise an older house makes at night.

When my alarm went off I was scrunched down around my pillows, my quilt clutched under my chin. I groaned and stretched as I got out of bed, working out the kinks. I threw on a robe and ran to Mom's and Dad's room, knocking quietly even though I wanted to wake them.

Dad had been up for a while. He had already showered and shaved, and Mom was sitting up in bed, hugging her knees. "You must be excited, too, Cary," she said, and grinned at me. "You know, the banquet's a sellout."

"This is not about the banquet," I said. I sat down on the edge of the bed and told them about my conversation with Mrs. Broussard.

I'll never forget the expressions on Mom's and Dad's faces. They went from surprise to fear to horror. When

Joan Lowery Nixon

I finished they still kept staring at me as if they were hoping I'd tell them it was all a bad dream.

Finally Dad said, "You heard Cragmore and Lamotta say that they killed Herb Gillian?"

"Not in so many words," I told him. "I didn't know what they meant."

Mom was suddenly on her knees. She crawled across the bed and wrapped her arms around me. "Charles!" she said. "They're planning to try to kill Cary!"

"We'll call Sergeant Slater," Dad said. He picked up the phone, but before he dialed the number he glanced over his shoulder and said, "Laura and Cary, you'd better get dressed."

Sergeant Slater arrived to take my statement. We were getting to know each other pretty well by now. He kept asking in different ways, "Did they give any indication of where this murder took place?"

"No," I said. "I didn't even know they were talking about a murder." I tried so hard to think if there could be anything else. There was a thought tickling the back of my brain, but I couldn't pull it out. Was there something else I should remember?

"Do you think Governor Milco is tied in with this?" Mom asked, but Dad shook his head.

"The construction kickbacks, yes," he said, "but not murder. Lamotta and Cragmore must have become involved in further graft. They're trying to protect themselves."

"Can you arrest them?" Mom asked.

"No," Sergeant Slater said. "We have no proof that

198

Herb Gillian has been murdered, or that Lamotta and Cragmore were even involved in his disappearance."

"Then what can we do?"

"They'll be questioned, as will Mrs. Broussard."

"What about Cary?"

"Don't worry about Cary," he said, but I don't think he convinced any of us.

"I'll cancel the banquet," Dad said.

"You can't!" I told him.

"Your daughter is right," Sergeant Slater said. "Just go on with your plans. You've hired extra security, there's the hotel security, too, and you'll have plenty of police protection. There shouldn't be any problems."

We kept our plans for the banquet, but there was no way I was going to school. Mom called the office and gave an excuse, not really telling them anything. At noon Justin telephoned to ask why I was missing classes.

"I can't tell you everything now," I said. "I will later."

"Are you all right?"

"I'm fine. Really." I was about as fine as anyone is who knows someone's out to kill her, but I couldn't tell Justin that.

"Are we still going to the banquet?" he asked.

"Sure," I answered. Sergeant Slater had said we'd be all right, hadn't he?

"What time should I pick you up?" Justin asked.

"Be here before seven-fifteen. We'll have a police escort, so we can't go in your car, Justin. We'll have to ride with Mom and Dad."

Mom came to the door and looked at me. "It's Justin,"

I mouthed. She looked less worried, but she didn't leave.

"I've got to go," I said. "I'll see you tonight."

I was okay during the rest of the day. It wasn't until I looked in the mirror and saw myself dressed in an almost new royal-blue silk dress with a string of pearls around my neck that I almost chickened out. What if I met up with the person who had tried to run me down and got Cindy instead? What if he were out there, waiting for me? The protection the police would give us couldn't be enough. Could it? My knees buckled, and I dropped down on my bedroom chair.

My eyes were drawn to the window that had been cut and repaired. I'd closed the curtains, so the pane of glass was covered, but I could almost see someone out there, climbing the tree, reaching out for the window.

I leaped out of my chair and ran downstairs to join the others. Wherever Mom and Dad were—that's where I wanted to be.

Justin arrived, looking great in a tux. We had only time to say hello when Dexter came in to tell us that the limo had arrived. Justin helped me into my coat, and we followed my parents and a couple of police officers out to a long white stretch limousine.

Normally, I would have enjoyed it. I've always loved limousines with their deep, plush seats and air of glamour. But tonight, as I climbed into the back seat I glanced toward the big broad-shouldered driver, his face in shadow, his cap over his eyes, and I shook right down to my toes.

I pushed at Justin, who bent over as he climbed in,

trying not to bump his head. "No!" I shouted. "We have to get out. This may be a trap!"

Dad held out a hand, restraining me. "What's the matter, Cary?" he asked.

"That driver," I said. "We don't know who he is. What if *they* sent him?"

The driver turned and held up a small leather case. Inside was a badge. "I'm with the Dallas police, ma'am," he told me.

I sunk back into my seat, as embarrassed as when I dropped a bowl of spaghetti in my lap during my tenth birthday party. Even more embarrassed. Everyone was looking at me.

They all spoke at once, trying to make things easier for me. "We'll make sure you've got protection," Mom said.

"You'll be all right, Cary," Dad said.

And Justin—dear old lovable Justin—said, "I don't know why you're so spooked, Cary, but don't worry. *I'll* take care of you."

When we arrived at the Adolphus, everything was a riot of red, white, and blue, and there were lots of reporters and camerapersons on hand. I looked for Sally Jo, but I didn't see her.

The chief of security, a lean, sharp-eyed, Clint Eastwood type, spoke to Sergeant Slater. I heard him say, "All my men have been alerted. We've been checking the guests, making sure each has an invitation."

"We'll put extra men inside the ballroom," the detective told him.

"It would help if we knew who we were looking for," the security chief said.

"We don't know," the detective answered. "For that matter, we don't know if we'll even have any problems tonight."

I gave a sigh of relief until the security chief added, "With a crowd like this—"

The two men nodded at each other, and I felt worse.

Dad and Mom were greeting people to the right and left as we made our way up the escalators to the lobby and then up the stairs to the ballroom's reception area.

Justin nudged me and said, "Smile. You're supposed to bow to the crowd and throw roses or something, I think."

"Very funny," I said, but I did try to smile and pretend that everything was fine and secure and there wasn't a killer somewhere out in that crowd.

We reached the ballroom. As one of the people in our group held open a door the noise of conversation and clinking dishes and glassware surged out like an explosion. The gigantic ballroom sparkled with candlelight, and the tables were bright with flowers and streamers. The banquet guests, who were elegantly dressed in tuxes and long gowns, were in their places. They rose when we arrived, and applauded as we filed to the head table.

"I hope they don't stare at us just because we're up here," Justin said as we sat down together. "If they do, I know I'm going to spill salad dressing on my shirt."

He didn't have to worry, because as soon as Dad had acknowledged the applause, everyone sat down and became busy with the salad course. A few people glanced idly at Justin and me, then went back to their salads and their conversation. It was Mom and Dad who interested them.

Some of the press had followed us into the room, and TV camerapersons were busy setting up their equipment. I spotted Sally Jo. She saw me, too, and came toward us, dodging one of the waiters. Because of the size of the large crowd, waiters and waitresses bustled about everywhere. An uncomfortable thought occurred to me.

As Sergeant Slater walked below the head table, I called to him and leaned across the table so he could hear me. "You've checked all the guests," I said, "but what about the waiters?"

"The waiters?" He did a slow turn, scanning the room.

"The hotel wouldn't have all these waiters constantly on staff," I said. "I bet they hired an extra number of waiters for tonight."

The detective motioned to the security chief, who came right over. "What's your procedure for hiring extra help for a banquet?"

"The event is listed, and people come by and apply."

"What do they need?"

"Experience and proof of citizenship or a green card."

"There's no special security check?"

"We've never needed more than that. The candidates or celebrities who come here arrange for extra security of their own, and I have a well-trained security staff."

"Does the hotel keep extra uniforms on hand?"

"Yes. In all sizes."

They looked at each other for just a second. Then the security chief said, "I'll get the employment list, although if you think someone has given a false name and false ID the names on the list won't help."

As Sally Jo reached the head table she stopped Sergeant Slater from leaving by grasping his arm. She said something to him, and they both turned toward the back of the room. A moment later she shrugged, said something else, and he left. She came to stand in front of me and grinned. "Working my way across the room was like going through an obstacle course."

"I need to talk to you," I told her.

A burst of laughter from a nearby table drowned out my words. "I said, I need to talk to you," I repeated.

At the same time Sally Jo practically shouted, "I didn't hear you."

There was so much I had to tell her. I pushed back my chair and stood up as I motioned to Sally Jo to come with me.

Mom stopped in mid-sentence, leaned across the woman who sat between us, and asked me, "Where are you going?"

"To the ladies' room," I mouthed. It was the truth. I thought Sally Jo and I would have a chance to talk there in private.

"I'll go with you," Mom said, but I shook my head and

gestured toward Sally Jo, who was waiting at the foot of the steps to the stage.

"I'll be with Sally Jo," I told Mom.

Mom looked a little dubious, but she nodded permission.

"See you in a few minutes," I said to Justin, who was hungrily digging into his second French roll, and joined Sally Jo.

We worked our way through the crowd, careful to dodge the waiters who were moving quickly.

As we left the noise of the ballroom we both stopped and took deep breaths. "These large banquets are noisier than football games," Sally Jo said. "Everybody has to scream to be heard."

There were only a couple of people in the upstairs reception area. A man stood near the stairs, looking down into the lobby, and I guessed he was one of the security people.

A woman walked across the area toward us, tucking a lipstick into a tiny handbag. "The rest rooms are probably over that way," I said, and as we walked toward them I repeated what Nora had told me.

Sally Jo stopped short. "You overheard them discussing a murder?"

As I nodded, she said, "The police will have to find the body to prove it. Where is it buried, Cary?"

Maybe it was because Sally Jo didn't ask if I knew but took it for granted that I did. The words came back to me. Quietly, I repeated exactly what I'd heard: "Because of his big mouth, he's up a creek." I clutched Sally Jo's arm. "John Lamotta said it, and then he laughed.

Joan Lowery Nixon

Sally Jo, I think the police will find Mr. Gillian's body buried in the creek bed near where they're building the freeway."

Sally Jo's eyes were huge. "Cary," she said, "this is the first time you've told this about the body to anyone, isn't it?"

"Yes," I said. "It just made sense to me right now."

Sally Jo glanced quickly around and pulled at my hand, tugging me back toward the ballroom. "We have to get you to a security guard or a policeman right away. You're the only witness . . . You're in more danger than you were before . . . If they knew . . ."

We were almost at the door to the ballroom when a waiter came out and made straight for us. He was a tall, muscular man, but his face was nondescript. So was his expression—a total blank. He carried a small metal tray down at his side but raised it as he stopped directly in front of us. "Sally Jo Wilson?" he asked, looking at both of us as though he were waiting to see which one would answer.

"Yes?" Sally Jo said.

"There's a phone call for you." The waiter nodded toward a door at the far side of the area. "You can take it in there."

The waiters working the ballroom were extra busy, but they weren't blind. They would have seen me when I came in. They would have known which one of us was Sally Jo. My heart started pounding, and I grabbed Sally Jo's arm. "Don't go," I screeched. "This guy's a fake."

"So I figured," Sally Jo answered, and she ordered, "Get out of our way."

206

He didn't budge. "Too bad for you," he said to her. "You had a chance to stay out of this." He moved the tray, and we could see the gun he was holding. I knew he could hear my heart. Now it was banging in my ears, and I could hardly breathe. This guy was going to kill us! "We're going to walk through the kitchen. Go ahead. Now." He made a little jab with his gun in that direction.

A waitress appeared behind him.

"Help us!" I managed to shout, but she wasn't one of the hotel waitresses. She was Francine.

"I spotted you," Sally Jo told her. "The security staff is looking for you."

"Let's get out of here fast," Francine said to the man. She made a grab for my arm.

If we left the hotel there was no doubt we'd be killed. If we stayed, at least we'd have a fighting chance.

And *fighting* was the word. I used Francine's momentum to swing her in front of me and into the guy holding the gun. And I kicked. I kicked hard, and as I heard the gun hit the floor I yelled and hit out at both of them. One punch landed so hard that a jolt of pain traveled from my hand to my shoulder, and I screamed, "Help! Somebody! Anybody! Help us!"

Sally Jo dove in, and I heard a crunching sound as her fist hit Francine's face. The man made a grab for my neck, but I twisted my head and bit down on his wrist, and he yelped and jerked his hand away. An elbow jabbed my ribs so hard that for a moment tears flooded my eyes and I couldn't see.

Suddenly someone grabbed my sore shoulder, trying

to pull me away. I struck out with my other hand and too late saw that it was Dexter. I gave him such a clip on the side of the head that he staggered backwards.

People yelled, and lights went off in my face.

I heard Dad saying, "Let go, Cary. Let go—*now!* Everything's under control." And I stopped fighting.

Dad helped me stand up, and as Mom brushed the hair from my eyes I could feel her fingers tremble. I watched the security chief and some of the undercover policemen lead Francine and the gunman from the room. They were surrounded by the newspaper and television people who tried to squeeze through the doors with them.

Dexter stood and rubbed his jaw.

"You're not a butler," I told him. "Who are you?"

"A bodyguard," Dad answered for him. "Your mother knew, but we were afraid you'd be frightened if you thought we had to have a bodyguard."

"You should have told me," I said. I looked at Dexter sheepishly. "At least before I socked Dexter. I'm sorry I hit you. I really am."

Dexter just smiled, but his jaw was beginning to swell. So was my right eye. I could feel it.

Some of Dad's staff began guiding the banquet guests back to their places, and I told Mom and Dad, "They were going to kill me. I remembered all of what I heard, and it finally made sense. I think I know where Herb Gillian's body is buried."

Sergeant Slater stepped forward. "We'll need an official statement," he said.

Chapter 19

I gave him a statement. I told him everything I knew, and I went over it all again for the crowd in the ballroom, as Don Franklin wanted me to do. And as I did, I explained how Sally Jo had helped me remember. I saw some of the cameras zoom in on her, and I hoped she'd get some of the attention she deserved from the news media.

I had kept my promise to Sally Jo. I gave everyone the facts, but the details—the background of the story —were just for her.

And when I'd finished I went back to the head table and said, "I want to go home, Dad."

Mr. Franklin, who was squatting to talk to him, said, "But it's time for your father to speak."

"Dad?" I pleaded.

"Dexter will see that you and Justin get home safely," Dad said and smiled. "You'll have lots of speeches to sit through if this campaign goes well."

A short time later, as Justin and I sat in the back seat of the limo, Dexter with the driver in the front seat, I told Justin, "It's all over, but I still feel shaky and scared."

"I feel a little scared of *you*," Justin said. "I didn't know you could fight like that." He put his right arm around my shoulder, and I winced, but I scooted over next to him.

"I don't know why your dad wants to go into politics," Justin told me. "My dad said that your dad is an idealist and idealists always think the impossible can happen."

"Correction," I said. "Idealists *make* the impossible happen."

We came to a boulevard stop. Justin bent down for a quick kiss, and we temporarily forgot about politics.

No matter how Justin and I felt about each other now, I knew that if Dad became governor, Justin would probably start dating someone else as soon as I moved to Austin. I had to admit to myself, I didn't want to be a hermit either. I'd begin dating other people, too.

But all that was somewhere in the future. What was happening right now was all that mattered, and right now, being here with Justin was exactly what I wanted.